CHOOSE YOUR OWN ADVENTURE®

ANTARCTICA!

BY LILY SIMONSON

ILLUSTRATED BY VLADIMIR SEMIONOV
COVER ILLUSTRATED BY IRIS MUDDY

CHOOSECO®
WAITSFIELD, VERMONT

Book design: Stacey Boyd, Big Eyedea Visual Design

For information regarding permission, write to:

CHOOSECO
P.O. Box 46
Waitsfield, Vermont 05673
www.cyoa.com

Publisher's Cataloging-in-Publication Data
Names: Simonson, Lily, author. | Semionov, Vladimir, illustrator. |
Muddy, Iris, illustrator.
Title: Antarctica! / Lily Simonson ; illustrated by Vladimir Semionov ;
cover illustrated by Iris Muddy..
Description: Waitsfield, VT : Chooseco, 2022. | 30 b&w illustrations. |
Series: Choose your own adventure. | Audience: Ages 9-12. | Summary:
This interactive adventure book places the reader in the position of a
young scientist who must choose between finishing an important experi-
ment and rescuing a colleague.
Identifiers: ISBN 9781954232099 (softcover)
Subjects: LCSH: McMurdo Station (Antarctica) -- Juvenile fiction. |
Decision making -- Juvenile fiction. | Scientists -- Juvenile fiction. |
Antarctica -- Juvenile fiction. | LCGFT: plot-your-own stories. | BISAC:
JUVENILE FICTION / Action & Adventure / General. | JUVENILE FICTION --
Interactive Adventures. | JUVENILE FICTION / Science & Nature /
General.
Classification: LCC PZ7.1 S566 2022 | [FIC]--dc22

Published simultaneously in the United States and Canada

Printed in Canada

10 9 8 7 6 5 4 3 2 1

For Sonora and Meadow

Special thanks to Jessica Stites, Dr. Joe Levy, Dr. Byron Adams, Dr. Jeff Marlow, Dr. Andrew Thurber, Dr. Becky Ball, Dr. Jill Mikucki, Dr. Victoria Orphan, Dr. John Priscu, Dr. Dale Anderson, Dr. Peter Girguis, Thomas Greene, Jay Dickson, and Elaine Hood.

BEWARE and WARNING!

This book is different from other books.

You and YOU ALONE are in charge of what happens in this story.

There are dangers, choices, adventures, and consequences. YOU must use all of your numerous talents and much of your enormous intelligence. The wrong decision could end in disaster—even death. But don't despair. At any time, YOU can go back and make another choice, alter the path of your story, and change its result.

YOU are a young scientist working in Antarctica. You're eager to get back to your research site to continue the experiment you began working on last year, when you suddenly receive word that one of your fellow scientists has gone missing. Do you join the search and rescue team, or do you head back to the research site and rescue your data and equipment from an impending flood? Whatever you choose, you will soon find yourself on an unexpected adventure that takes you through the frozen Antarctic landscape . . . watch out for the aliens!

The wind nearly pushes you over as you heave yourself up into the helicopter.

"Can I squeeze in here?" you ask. The two other passengers nod. You feel a rush of excitement as the propellers rev up. You can hardly wait to get to your research site at Lake Bonney.

You are the youngest scientist in Antarctica, but also the most celebrated. As an expert research scuba diver, you have made discoveries in Antarctica's ice-covered lakes and oceans that have changed the world's understanding of how life can exist in the most extreme environments on Earth, and possibly on other planets.

You have now turned your attention to the extraordinary microscopic animals that thrive in Antarctica's dry, frigid soils. Antarctica's land is so inhospitable to life that the continent's apex predator is in fact a microscopic worm—the nematode *Scottnema lindsayae*. These creatures can essentially freeze-dry themselves for long periods of time—nobody even knows how long!—and then reanimate when conditions improve. You began an experiment last year to understand this mysterious process, known as biostasis. If you don't get back to your research site very soon you will lose all your data.

Suddenly, the whir reverses and the propellers cut out.

"Stand by!" The helicopter pilot's voice crackles through the intercom speaker in your helmet.

Turn to the next page.

You look out the window. A familiar figure rushes toward the helicopter pad. It's Jordan, your best friend and the supervisor of scuba-diving operations in Antarctica. She pokes her head into the helicopter cabin and you all remove your helmets so you can hear her. She turns to you.

"We have a search and rescue starting. A scientist, Amir Burman, missed his check-in. No sign of him when they did a flyover. The good news is that we have picked up a signal we think is coming from his radio. The bad news is that the signal is coming from a spot out in the middle of the sea ice," explains Jordan.

You're familiar with Dr. Burman's work. He is a prominent figure in the field of Antarctic marine biology. He is also an accomplished diver. But if he has disappeared under the sea ice, his chances of survival are minuscule. You brace yourself. You know what she's about to say.

Go on to the next page.

"Please come with us. I feel like you're our only hope for finding him," your friend states.

Jordan's right. The body of water adjacent to the research station, McMurdo Sound, is covered by the largest expanse of sea ice in the world. Diving beneath it can be dangerous, and you and Jordan are by far the most experienced Antarctic scuba divers.

There's one problem. If you don't take this flight to your research site, the past year of research will be ruined—and with it, most of your career as an Antarctic scientist. Satellite images show that unprecedented ice melt will soon flood the equipment. You've got to get back there to save the gear and download the data. You are the only one who knows how to monitor this experiment properly. Your entire lab back at home is counting on you.

If you decide to join the search party for Amir Burman, turn to the next page.

If you decide to travel to your research site, turn to page 13.

4

You sigh and look at Jordan. "Of course I'll go with you."

"I knew I could count on you." Jordan turns to the pilot. "Think you can make a pit stop?"

"Not a problem," the pilot shouts. "We'll drop you at New Harbor before continuing on to Lake Bonney."

Your experiment is most likely ruined. But as Jordan collapses into the seat next to you, you catch her nervous expression. There is a life at stake here.

Besides, you would do anything for Jordan. She is the entire reason you came to Antarctica and made your historic discoveries. You became friends when you were training to become a research scuba diver. Jordan was your instructor, and she shared amazing stories from her work overseeing scuba-diving operations at McMurdo Station in Antarctica. You were dazzled by her tales of the unique landscape beneath the sea ice, and resolved then and there to become an Antarctic scientist so you could experience this world in person. In the past three years, you and Jordan have become almost inseparable.

The helicopter crew heaves the search-and-rescue gear into the cargo area of the helicopter. You all buckle back in and the pilot takes off toward the signal. You peer out the window at the sea ice below. There is no evidence of any activity as you land on the helicopter pad next to New Harbor Camp.

Turn to page 6.

You begin to administer CPR to Jordan as the helicopter takes off above you. Her breath starts to return, but her exhalations carry the same noxious smell as the backpack. You begin to feel dizzy. Are you breathing in the same fumes that have incapacitated Jordan? Gradually, everything goes black.

Sitting up slowly, you realize that you are back at the research station. *How did I get here? How long have I been asleep?* you wonder.

The station doctor appears before you. "Welcome back. You and Jordan have been out for days. The helicopter pilot found you both unconscious on the ice."

"Is . . . is Jordan okay?" you stammer.

"She came to about an hour ago. She's groggy, but otherwise doing fine. We've run a toxicology screen on both of you but can't seem to identify what caused your brief coma."

"Did they find Dr. Burman?"

"I'm afraid he's still missing."

You feel fatigued for days but gradually your energy returns. Eventually you are well enough to head to your field site, but as you expected, too much time has passed and your experiment is ruined. Both your research and rescue efforts have failed. You return home, dejected.

The End

6

You briefly search the camp, but the Jamesway—a semipermanent, elongated hut—is empty. You and Jordan next head out onto the frozen ocean surface. You drag your dive gear across the sea ice until you reach the area where the radio signal is originating. You scan the ice. "I don't see anything," you say to your friend. But as you turn toward Jordan, you notice some debris about six feet away. "Wait. Look." You move aside some loose chunks of ice to reveal a small backpack. It must be the source of Dr. Burman's radio signal!

Jordan reaches over to pick up the backpack but then drops it. "Ugh," she says. "That smell is making me dizzy. Let's seal this thing up and look at it back at the station." Even a few feet away, the smell overwhelms you—it's like burning rubber mixed with formaldehyde.

You pull out an extra-large sample bag. But just as you reach toward the backpack, you catch a glimpse of a strange-looking metallic object inside. You peer closer.

"I don't know, Jordan," you say. "I see something weird in there. I think it could lead us to Dr. Burman."

If you seal the backpack in a plastic sample bag and wait until you are back at the station to examine it, turn to page 9.

If you sort through the backpack to look for clues, turn to page 21.

Jordan pulls out a thick sample bag and you deposit the backpack inside and seal it up. As you are taping the bag shut, a bright spot in the distance catches your eye. There is an orange glow emanating from a crack in the sea ice. "Jordan, look!"

"What *is* that?" Jordan exclaims.

"I think we better take a closer look." You approach the crack and peer down into the water. There is some sort of light below the surface! As quickly as you can, you and Jordan don your weights, tanks, and drysuits—waterproof suits that protect you from the below-freezing water.

You take a deep breath and climb into the crack. You exhale and sink down, enveloped on all sides by the six feet of sea ice that cover the McMurdo Sound. Letting more air out of your drysuit, you lower yourself farther until you are finally below the sea ice.

Turn to the next page.

Descending beneath the sea ice is like entering another universe. The top surface of the ice is opaque white, but its translucent underside is home to colonies of single-celled algae, known as diatoms. The sunlight filters through the diatom-rich ice, transforming it into a glowing rainbow of gold, neon green, and turquoise. You are surrounded by a cathedral of giant luminous icicles, frozen in the shapes of branching tree roots, upside-down ice cream cones, and feather boas. Known as brinicles, these ice tubes are created by channels of briny seawater. Heavy with extra salt, the briny tendrils sink below the fresher water, then freeze on the outside.

Turn to page 12.

12

It is spring and the sun is finally circling above the horizon. But during the preceding winter months, it was dark around the clock, so now there is hardly any plankton in the water column. This means that the visibility at this time of year is unparalleled—you can see ten times farther than in any other ocean on the planet. It feels like you're not even in water; as your fins propel you forward, it's like you're flying through the air.

The orange light catches your eye again and snaps you back into focus. You realize it's receding at a rapid pace.

You check behind you and see Jordan lingering at the crack in the ice where you entered. She signals that she needs to add more weights to her drysuit and begins ascending back to the surface. To follow protocol, you *must* wait for your partner. But even through these crystal-clear Antarctic waters, the light is disappearing quickly from view.

If you decide to prioritize safety protocols and wait for your partner, turn to page 17.

If you decide to follow the orange light, turn to page 23.

You catch yourself holding your breath as the helicopter crosses over the McMurdo Sound and flies toward the exquisite landscape of Taylor Valley. Taylor is one of the McMurdo Dry Valleys—one of the harshest, driest deserts on the planet. Unlike most of Antarctica, the Dry Valleys are mostly free of ice and snow. Still, giant glaciers and glowing icy lakes punctuate the dramatic valleys. Each time you come here, you find yourself more awestruck by the landscape. There is nothing else like it. The air is so clear that it feels like you can see forever.

The helicopter descends on the landing pad next to Lake Bonney—a huge ice-covered lake surrounded by steep valley walls. At Lake Bonney, you work closely with two other scientists, Nia and Lucas. Though you are running separate experiments and come from different institutions, you are all currently studying the nematode *Scottnema lindsayae*.

While nematodes all over the world can put themselves into biostasis, you discovered that this Antarctic species has a unique and extremely powerful ability to enter this state of suspended animation. But the details remain mysterious. You feel sure that you are on the verge of unlocking its secrets, but you could be thwarted by warming trends in Antarctica.

Scottnema is very well-adapted to the soils of the Dry Valleys. However, higher temperatures mean more glacial melt. These changes to *Scottnema*'s habitat mean that another species of nematode is beginning to take over, which poses a threat to the formerly dominant worm.

Turn to the next page.

"Hey, let me take that," says Nia as you approach camp, nodding at the bag in your hand. "Lucas and I will set up camp while you take care of your equipment." You toss your pack over to her with a hurried thank you. Nia and Lucas know that you are in a big rush to save your equipment from the unprecedented meltwater.

When you arrive, you see that a new stream has carved a path leading toward your experiment site. You will have to change the way you weatherproof from now on. Your equipment is set up to be protected from dust and snow. But models predict that the weather patterns in Antarctica will change drastically in the near future. In addition to increased wetness from glacial melt, Antarctica could even begin to see rain for the first time in more than 115,000 years. It's time to update your gear. Everything must be 100 percent watertight going forward. Luckily, you got there just in time to retrieve all your data.

You breathe a sigh of relief as you walk back toward camp and give a high five to Nia and Lucas. The three of you worked together at Lake Bonney last year, too. You get to know a person really well when they are the only human for miles around and you spend almost every waking moment with them, even if it's only for a few weeks at a time. Nia is a total goofball and Lucas is constantly throwing puns at you. They keep you laughing, that's for sure.

Go on to the next page.

Your campmates have unpacked the kitchen and lab gear, but you still have to pitch your own tent. Each year, you set it up in the same "lucky spot," next to a mummified seal that everyone has nicknamed Carla. Penguins and seals occasionally wander from the coast up into the Dry Valleys and get stranded. The cold, dry air preserves their bodies almost perfectly. Most of them have been there for decades or even centuries, and scientists often use them as landmarks.

Lucas walks by and greets Carla. "I thought of a good riddle. What do you call a pregnant seal in the Dry Valleys?"

"What?"

"A mummy to be!" Lucas laughs so hard at his own joke he can barely finish the punchline. You roll your eyes but cannot help but chuckle too.

After you're all set up, you meet Lucas and Nia in the Jamesway—a large semicircular tent-like structure that houses your makeshift kitchen. You usually take turns cooking meals, but on the first night the three of you decide to cook together.

Before eating, you radio McMurdo Station for your daily check-in. They tell you to make sure everything is secured, as an extreme windstorm is expected.

Turn to the next page.

16

"I wonder if we can make it down to the valley for the Thanksgiving party before the storm hits," says Nia. Last year you started calling her the Chief Morale Officer because she always sniffs out the fun.

You had almost forgotten that tomorrow was Thanksgiving. Being far from your families over the holidays can be tough, so everyone in Antarctica puts in a lot of effort to make them extra joyful.

"We can make a call in the morning," says Lucas.

You say goodnight and crawl into your tent. Even though you are exhausted, your mind is racing with excitement about getting back to your experiment here. Eventually you drift off.

You wake with a jump to voices outside your tent. In Antarctic summer, the sun never sets, so it's impossible to tell day from night. You suppose it must be morning so you check your watch. It's only 2:00 AM! Who is awake at this hour?

Turn to page 18.

You check your watch. Only five minutes pass while Jordan adjusts her gear, but it feels like an eternity. She finally reappears and you lead her toward the light, which has almost disappeared. All of a sudden, a tug jerks you backward. Something has grabbed hold of your scuba tank! You struggle against it but find yourself pulled down.

You turn to see that Jordan is being pulled down alongside you. You freeze in terror for a long moment before realizing you can escape if you drop your air supply and unclick from your tank. You reach over to free yourself and signal Jordan to do the same, but she shakes her head. She gestures toward the crack, which is receding quickly. You may not be able to make it back there in one breath.

If you choose to keep your tank on and let yourself be dragged backward, turn to page 35.

If you unclip yourself from your tank and make a break for the surface, turn to page 43.

You don't like to cavesdrop, but you're annoyed at being awoken so you strain to hear the voices that disturbed you. It sounds like another language. *Spanish? Italian!* But why would anybody be speaking Italian?

You unzip the window of your tent to take a look. One figure has their back to you but the other one you see very clearly, and it's a face you've never seen before. A paralyzing chill runs through your body. Who is in your camp? You know everyone who works in Taylor Valley. How could there be somebody here you don't recognize? It's impossible!

The two figures are struggling with a large orange bag. Eventually they lift the bag together and start to walk up the hill and around the ridge.

Where could they possibly be going at 2:00 AM? You need to stop them! Or at least find out what's going on. You feel deeply spooked and you want to get Nia and Lucas. But if you don't start following them now, you might never catch up. You struggle out of your sleeping bag and into your wind pants and hiking boots, trying to decide what to do.

If you decide to go wake the other scientists, turn to page 28.

If you decide to follow the two mysterious figures on your own, turn to page 47.

"I really think we need to check this out now," you insist. You pull out the thickest mittens you have and reach toward the backpack, but Jordan grabs your wrist.

"Let me do it. You came out here to help me with the search; I owe you a favor."

Jordan puts on her own mittens and begins emptying the bag. So far everything she pulls out is ordinary gear, but it all radiates that same noxious smell. Jordan starts to pull out the strange metal object, when suddenly she drops to the ground.

You rush over to her. Jordan is unconscious. She has a pulse, but she's not breathing. Why didn't you listen to her and just seal the bag?

This is my fault, you think.

Looking toward New Harbor Camp, you see that the helicopter is still on the pad. You grab your radio. "Please, I need help! Is anyone there? Can anyone hear me?"

You can tell that something's wrong . . . your signal isn't going through. In horror you realize your radio has gotten wet, perhaps from the substance in the pack. You start to feel lightheaded yourself. Jordan was obviously exposed to something poisonous. You need that helicopter to take her to the doctor back at McMurdo. But in the meantime, you've got to keep her alive!

If you decide to run toward the helicopter to try to get their attention, turn to page 26.

If you choose to administer CPR to Jordan right away and continue to try your radio, turn to page 5.

You may have just torpedoed your career by proceeding solo. But something tells you that you simply cannot lose track of the light. You clip a tether to the rope that connects you to the surface so that Jordan can track you as you swim toward the light.

The light continues over a steep drop-off and then disappears. You spin around, searching for it, when something else catches your eye. You swim past the drop-off, and all of a sudden the seafloor opens up to reveal the most extraordinary sight.

Before you lies a giant microbial mat—a fuzzy community of single-celled bacteria that often forms on the seafloor where sulfur or methane seep from beneath the Earth's crust. Most mats on the seafloor are white, yellow, or orange. But this one seems to pulsate and shine with every color on the spectrum, almost like a prism.

You pull out a bag to collect a sample when you feel a tug on your tether. More than a tug—you are being pulled. At last you see Jordan, signaling you to return to the surface. You hesitate. But her wild arm movements suggest to you that something may be seriously wrong. Reluctantly, you swim back to the surface.

Turn to the next page.

You've hardly had a chance to take your first breath when you hear Jordan say, "The missing scientist was found!"

"*What?*" you say. "Where? How?" You climb out of the water, then lie flat on your back on the cold ice as you catch your breath.

"I don't know yet. Apparently he had multiple radio failures that are still being investigated."

You consider this as you slowly get to your feet. "Jordan, I need you to come back down with me. There's something you should see."

"Are you joking? We only have twenty minutes before the helicopter comes back for us!"

"Jordan, this is a big deal." You nod to her to head back to the water with you. Time is short but you've got to get a sample of that microbial mat.

Jordan heaves a sigh. "Fine. But you better be right about this. After you."

You dive into the water and retrace your strokes, shivering with excitement, as Jordan follows close behind.

You swim over the drop-off and your breath catches as you see the vibrant, fuzzy microbial mat emerge. Except something is wrong—you can see bits of it fading before your eyes. It seems to be dying right in front of you. How strange! You pull out your sample bag and scoop some in. You and Jordan hustle back to the surface. You shake with excitement as you wriggle out of your tank and drysuit. While you missed out on saving your Lake Bonney experiment, this discovery feels like it could be extraordinary.

Go on to the next page.

Back at the station, you begin studying your sample. None of the microbes in the sample are at all related to anything you've seen before. There are not just one, but half a dozen new species. You immediately share your findings with colleagues online.

The next morning, you open the door to your lab to find that it is already occupied. A man in a dark suit is ransacking your work bench.

"Excuse me?" you say, trying to sound calm.

"Ah! This must be it." The man holds up what is left of the microbial mat sample. "I'm Agent Combs, CIA. I'm afraid I have to confiscate this sample and order you to pause your research on it. It's a national security issue."

You are stunned. How could this possibly be? "What?! I can't let you take that!" you cry.

"I'm afraid you don't have a choice." Before you know it, he's gone. You feel tears welling up. Then you realize that you still have the GPS coordinates. You can go back to collect more. This time, you'll wait a while to share your discoveries.

You arrange to head back to the strange microbial mat later that morning. But when you return to the dive site to collect samples, the mat has disappeared. You spend the rest of your career searching for similar microbial colonies, but never find anything like it again.

The End

You look up to see the pilot stepping back into the helicopter. You run as fast as you can, waving your arms wildly. The wind is blowing against you, and you feel like you are running in slow motion. Your stomach sinks as you watch the helicopter lift off the ground. Suddenly it pauses in midair, hovers, then reverses course. They see you!

The helicopter touches down again, its propellers clicking off.

"Please, I need your help!" you shout. "It's Jordan, she was hurt, or exposed to a poison—I don't know what happened but she's not breathing. We have to get her back to McMurdo!"

The pilot hops down out of the helicopter. "Lead the way," she says to you without missing a beat.

Go on to the next page.

You lead the pilot back to Jordan. Thankfully, she is breathing again. But she remains unconscious. The two of you drag her to the helicopter and heave her into it. As you climb back down, a wave of heartache washes over you. You feel like this is your fault. If you had just sealed up the bag and looked at it back at the station, this would not have happened. You cannot imagine leaving Jordan's side now. You do not trust the remaining helicopter passengers to give proper CPR if she needs it.

At the same time, you feel certain that the mysterious backpack lying on the ice holds the clue to finding the missing scientist. There is no time to waste if something happened to him out there on the sea ice. *Or under the sea ice*, you think suddenly.

You are not supposed to dive solo. But this could be an emergency that requires it.

If you tell the pilot you're going to stay behind, turn to page 52.

If you return to the research station with the helicopter to make sure Jordan is okay, turn to page 60.

28

You emerge clumsily from your tent and head toward Nia's. "Nia! Nia, wake up!" No response. *Is she even in there? Is she just a really good sleeper?*

You don't want to barge in, so you move on to Lucas's tent. "Lucas! There were strangers in our camp!" You hear a rustling in the tent.

"What?" says a sleepy voice. At least somebody will reply to you!

"I saw two people in our camp that I didn't recognize. They just took off up the valley. They had an orange bag stuffed to the brim."

Lucas pokes his head out. "That's impossible."

"I know it sounds crazy, but I swear. We've got to try to catch up with them."

"You must have been dreaming. There's nobody else out here. Let's go back to sleep."

"Fine." You turn and walk away, thinking about what to do. You are starting to feel really freaked out. You feel a shiver, like you're being watched. You turn around and see Lucas's face peering at you from his tent window. He ducks down when you catch his eye. If he was so desperate to go back to sleep, why is he still up, staring at you like that? You realize you'll never be able to rest if you don't try to catch up with those intruders. If you get over the next ridge, you'll probably be able to see them again. But is it wise to strike out from camp by yourself with a storm moving in?

If you stay behind and wait till morning to investigate, turn to page 30.

If you decide to follow the mystery pair, turn to page 55.

After a fitful night's sleep, you pull yourself warily out of your tent. When you enter the Jamesway, Nia and Lucas are cooking breakfast.

"Happy Thanksgiving!" they say. With all the confusion from last night, Thanksgiving was the last thing on your mind. But your mood lightens right away when you see their outfits. They are both wearing feather boas and neon wigs. Nia is wearing a sequined cape and Lucas is wearing an old ball gown. Goofy costumes are your favorite Antarctic holiday tradition.

"We don't think it's a good idea to risk hiking down the valley for the party. Even if we make it before the storm hits, we might not be able to make it back to Lake Bonney for several days. Our experiments would be destroyed. So we're going to have our own celebration," says Lucas.

"Sounds great!" you say, rummaging through the costume box for something silly. You get so engrossed in piecing together your costume that you almost forget about the night before. As you don some oversized sunglasses and lederhosen, you catch Lucas staring at you and wonder if he's even bothered to tell Nia about what happened last night.

"We need to talk about the intruders," you say.

"Oh yeah, Lucas told me you had a dream you saw some people in our camp last night. Spooky!"

"It wasn't a dream! And we have to figure out who they were."

"It's totally normal to have super vivid dreams here. They call them false awakenings. I think it's the twenty-four-hour sunlight," says Lucas.

Turn to page 32.

"Why aren't you taking this seriously? Somebody was in our camp!"

"Let's just have breakfast and get to work." Nia tries to sound reassuring, but her voice seems tense. "Once we settle in, you'll realize everything is totally normal. Well, as normal as it can be in Antarctica."

"Besides," says Lucas, "what can we do? There's a major storm coming in. We've only got a few hours to move our experiments forward before we're stuck in our tents for days on end."

He's right. Even though it's a holiday, you all have work to do. After breakfast Nia and Lucas head out to gather samples. You can't shake the nagging suspicion that Lucas, and maybe even Nia, are hiding something. Neither one seemed the least bit curious about the intruders in camp.

You double check to make sure Nia and Lucas are out of view and then quickly slip inside their lab. Everything seems pretty normal. You begin opening drawers. Standard beakers, flasks, soil samples. Feeling anxious, you start to leave when your foot catches on a black case on the floor. It has a combination lock on it, but it's wedged partway open. You bend forward and lift the lid to find . . . stacks of cash? But the bills are colorful, definitely not green dollar bills. You lean closer and realize they are euros. More money than you can even wrap your head around. *A briefcase full of cash? What is this, a James Bond movie?*

Go on to the next page.

You move the briefcase and underneath it you see a packet of papers. You bend closer to read the title: *Preliminary Findings: Inducing Biostasis in Advanced Organisms*. You start to thumb through the pages when the sound of footsteps stops you in your tracks. It really does feel like you're stuck in an action film. You fling open a cabinet and climb in, straining to peek out through the slats.

Lucas walks in first, dragging a heavy orange bag. Nia follows, pushing the other end inside. They unzip it and you see . . . a mummified penguin!

Turn to the next page.

"This one is just stuck in biostasis. Paolo and I tried all night to reanimate it."

"I have some more samples we can pull from. Maybe that will help."

What? Who is Paolo? Were he and Nia the figures from last night? And what did Nia mean when she said the penguin was "stuck in biostasis"? Secretly experimenting on protected wildlife is completely unethical. Not to mention bioprospecting! Do they have a permit for this?

For years, pharmaceutical companies have approached you about transferring the nematode's biostasis mechanisms to more advanced organisms, and ultimately humans. But you always saw that as violating the spirit of the Antarctic Treaty's Madrid Protocol, which dictates that Antarctica should be a sanctuary set aside for basic science only.

Nia and Lucas put the bag down. Lucas picks up a box of vials and holds it up to the light. They open the door and exit the hut with the box. You obviously need to notify the National Science Foundation representative at McMurdo right away. But you can hardly believe what you've seen. You want to talk to Nia and Lucas to try to get the full story. Yet you no longer trust them.

If you report their activities directly to the National Science Foundation representative, turn to page 98.

If you confront Nia and Lucas, turn to page 108.

You grab Jordan's hand, signaling her to stay with you. Your heart is racing. You're risking not just your life, but Jordan's too. Yet your gut tells you that you'll soon find Dr. Burman.

You try to stay calm and keep your breathing steady as you are pulled further and further away from the crack at the surface. Suddenly you find yourselves shoved through some sort of airlock and onto . . . dry land! Thrust out of the buoyancy of the ocean, you stumble forward onto your face. You pull your regulator out and find that you can indeed breathe freely. You are inside a large cylindrical chamber that is filled with air, not water.

Turn to the next page.

36

Looking up, you see the missing scientist, Dr. Amir Burman, standing over you. You turn toward the outside of the chamber and see a group of glowing orange oblong figures. You try to make out more details, but the orange light radiating from them is so bright that your eyes cannot focus on them.

"What is happening?" you ask, your head spinning. "What are those . . . things?"

"I'm glad you're sitting down for this," says Dr. Burman. "Those things are . . . well, aliens. From Europa."

"Aliens? Europa?" you repeat dimly. Your eyes are glued to the creatures surrounding you outside the chamber. Is this a hallucination? Just one day ago you were minding your own business on what you know to be the only inhabited planet in the solar system. But you suppose that's still true, since Europa is technically one of Jupiter's moons, and not actually a planet.

Turn to page 38.

38

"We call it Pyrath," interrupts a strange robotic voice. You look around and notice the voice is coming from a small box. It appears to be an intercom. You and Jordan look nervously from the intercom to Dr. Burman, then back to the intercom.

"It's some sort of artificial intelligence translation device," says Dr. Burman. "That's how I've been communicating with them."

You always believed that if other life did exist in our solar system, humans would find it on Jupiter's moon, Europa. Europa may contain many of life's essential building blocks, as its icy surface appears to cover a vast saltwater ocean. But you never expected that the life on Europa would be intelligent, or that *it* would find *you*.

"The Pyrathians want to build a small research station of their own here on Earth," says Dr. Burman. "They have come to the Antarctic because the ice-covered terrain here is very similar to their homeland. But they need our help."

"Your planet is in pain," crackles the voice in the intercom. You see one of the orange glowing figures standing near you, just outside the chamber. "Yes. We came here because we wanted to study your planet, especially the icy seas that remind us of Pyrath. It is even more beautiful and fascinating than we could have imagined. We want to stay here permanently. But we see that Earth is on the verge of dangerous collapse and will soon be inhospitable to us—and maybe even to you, too. Humans release too many gases that trap heat in the atmosphere. The ocean will soon be too warm for us."

Go on to the next page.

You know this, only too well. At the current rate, there will be places on Earth that will become too hot to support even human life in a few decades. You put your hands over your face, still trying to wrap your head around what's happening.

"But the Pyrathians have a plan to help us stop global warming. Even reverse it!"

Dr. Burman leads you over to an aquarium-like object on the other side of the chamber, filled with seawater. Leaning in, you see that the bottom of the tank is lined with the most beautiful fuzzy iridescent growths you've ever seen. "This tank is a bioreactor filled with chemosynthetic microbes from Pyrath. The Pyrathians are using it to run experiments."

You and Jordan try to take all this in.

"Experiments? Chemosynthetic? What are you talking about?" Jordan asks. You sometimes forget that she has not studied microbiology.

"Let me explain it like this," says Dr. Burman. "Deep underwater creatures that don't get any sunlight need to use something called chemosynthesis to get enough energy to grow. It's like photosynthesis in plants. But in this case, instead of sunlight, the energy comes from chemicals."

"It makes sense that chemosynthesis would be the basis of life on Europa, or Pyrath, since it is so far from the sun," you add.

Turn to page 41.

"Exactly," says Dr. Burman. "The Pyrathians say that the microbes they have brought here from Pyrath can consume sulfur, ammonium, carbon dioxide, and methane more efficiently than any organism on Earth. It could completely fix our climate, and even reverse some of the global warming trends we've seen already."

"Well, what do they want us for?" you reply. "Why don't they just release it?"

The artificial intelligence voice interjects again through the intercom. "Our microbe is too sensitive to sunlight. Pyrath is eight times as far from the sun as your Earth. These microbes would need to grow throughout the Antarctic Ocean, including areas exposed to sunlight. We know there are microbes in the lakes here that have developed special protection against your radiation from the sun. Dr. Burman says that they are called cyanobacteria. We want to combine them with our microbes from Pyrath. The cyanobacteria would benefit our microbes and vice versa."

"But the Pyrathians cannot survive out of water long enough to collect the cyanobacteria from the lakes," says Dr. Burman. "They need us to do it. I want to help them, but I don't know how to pull it off at this point. By now, the whole station is probably looking for me."

Turn to the next page.

Jordan frowns. "Wait. Even if the Pyrathians are telling the truth, this could totally backfire. First of all, the Antarctic Treaty forbids us from introducing any species that are not native to Antarctica. Let alone any species not native to planet Earth! New microbes would change the entire ecosystem here in Antarctica, and possibly all over the world. Besides, climate change is a problem we humans created. We cut down countless forests. We burned fossil fuels. We factory farmed. We can't just sit back and expect a microbe to fix it," Jordan finishes.

"But Jordan," Dr. Burman replies, "even if we switch everything to a sustainable system today, there is still no proven way to significantly reduce the greenhouse gases we have already released. The Pyrathian microbes have the potential to reverse many of humanity's impacts on the environment. This could be our chance to . . . well, save the planet."

Jordan has been edging toward the bioreactor and eyeing the microbial mat inside with a strange look on her face. You see that it can easily be destroyed with a single cut to the film around it. You can't see her hand, but you suspect she has her dive knife ready. You trust Jordan's instincts, but the possibility of stabilizing the climate is making your entire body buzz with hope.

If you stop Jordan and try to help the aliens, turn to page 56.

If you allow Jordan to destroy the bioreactor, turn to page 68.

The crack where you entered is easily 1,000 feet away, and once you detach from your tank, you'll have only one breath to get back there. Jordan is shaking her head no, but you feel sure you both can make it. You lock eyes with Jordan and signal her to fill her lungs. You unclip your tanks in unison and drop your regulators.

You kick as fast as you can while still preserving your breath. But when you turn to check on Jordan, you notice that she's lagging way behind. You double back and grab her.

She's clearly running out of air, so you swim as quickly as you can. Yet you know your swift flight is putting you both in a new kind of danger. When scuba divers ascend too rapidly, dangerous bubbles of nitrogen form in the bloodstream. The bubbles cause decompression sickness, known as "the bends." And the bends can be fatal.

You finally reach the opening and push Jordan up to the surface before climbing out yourself.

"What on Earth was *that*?" you say when you've finally caught your breath.

Jordan's eyes widen. "I've never seen anything like it." She's lying on her back, her breath shallow.

"I wish we could go back and check it out, but there's no way we can dive again after that ascent."

Jordan agrees. "Maybe I'm imagining it, but I'm feeling bent already."

The symptoms of the bends usually take some time to set in, but you are also already feeling tingly and woozy. You may have an extreme case.

Turn to the next page.

"We definitely need to get back to the station and into the chamber." The hyperbaric chamber at McMurdo Station will dissolve the nitrogen bubbles that formed during your ascent before they can do long-term damage.

"Jordan to McMurdo Station," she says into her radio, sitting up slowly. "We need a medevac helicopter."

You grimace and put your head in your hands. "The rescue team is not supposed to need a rescue. How can we ever explain what just happened? Will anyone believe us?"

"Probably not," says Jordan.

On the way home you fight back a carsick feeling as the helicopter hugs the surface of the sea ice. It's important to fly low. An increase in altitude could make your decompression sickness fatal.

Upon landing, you want to meet right away with Alex Miles, the station manager, to tell him about what you experienced.

"No way," says Jordan. "We need to go straight to the chamber." You sigh, but you know she's right.

Your session in the hyperbaric chamber seems endless, but finally you and Jordan get clearance from the doctor to leave. You immediately head over to Alex's office. When you explain what happened, Alex gives you a strange look. His mouth is open, yet he doesn't seem as surprised as you expected him to be. You barely believe your *own* story. Why is he so calm?

Go on to the next page.

"We've got to get divers back there immediately to see what this thing is," you say.

Jordan stops you. "Don't you think that's a bit dangerous?"

"Maybe, but we need to figure out what's happening. And what about Dr. Burman?"

"Sorry, but I'm with Jordan," says Alex. "There's no way I'm going to send any of our divers back there. You were attacked! It's obviously too dangerous. I'm calling in the Navy."

Because of an incoming storm, naval support will not arrive for another two days. While you wait, the missing scientist mysteriously reappears back at New Harbor Camp. He says he simply had a communications malfunction, but all is well.

The Navy finally arrives, and you guide their divers to the place under the ice where you were attacked. But there is no sign of your attacker.

Jordan tells everyone you saved her life. You receive a medal of honor for your heroism, and the promise of future funding to continue your experiment at Lake Bonney. You almost feel ashamed accepting the accolades. Jordan's life would not have been at risk in the first place if you had not led her on a foolish chase through a crack in the sea ice.

The End

You put on your brown jacket rather than the standard-issue red parka—you want to stay camouflaged. You throw a walkie-talkie radio into your pack along with some food and water, then set off toward the next ridge. Just as you reach the top, you see the figures in the distance. The valley around Lake Bonney is incredibly steep, carved by ancient glaciers. With your quick pace, you gain on them, but you don't want to get too close.

After tailing the two figures for about half an hour, you see them turn toward you as they stop for a break. The landscape is littered with giant ventifacts—boulders ten times your size, sculpted by the extreme wind into intricate forms, full of Swiss cheese–like holes in all manner of shapes. You duck behind one for cover. But it may be too late. When you peer over the top, they seem to be standing there watching for you. Ugh! They must have seen you, because now they have started walking again and they are moving much more quickly. They are heading straight for Hughes Glacier.

You pick up the pace and go after them. You are so close! You arrive at the base of Hughes Glacier and start walking alongside it. Just as you are about to catch up to them, they seem to disappear into thin air. You pause and look around. You hear a strange sound. Voices? No, not voices. A loud echoing creak. The glacier is calving—a huge chunk of ice has broken off the top and is falling toward you! It feels like it's all happening in slow motion. You dive away from the glacier as quickly as you can, but that hideous sound follows you.

Turn to the next page.

48

You feel a jolt of pain in your leg. You look down and see it stuck beneath a large glacial boulder. You lean forward to try to free yourself, but the ice is too heavy. You're stuck, and badly injured. Your leg throbs, and pain surges through your body. You pull your backpack on top of you to find the radio and call for help. But just as you click it on, you hear another sound.

"Wait!" This time it's definitely a human voice, not a chunk of ice tumbling off a glacier.

You look up, feeling terrified. "Hello?" You crane your neck around and see the stranger that was in your camp. You realize his companion is Nia!

"Hi there," says Nia. She kneels down next to you. "I'm glad you're alive. We saw what happened." She feels your pulse and touches your head. "You're in shock. Let's breathe together."

"Nia!" The pain is taking over again and you can barely speak. "What is going on? Who is that?" You gesture at the stranger.

He steps closer, nodding, and says something to Nia in Italian. "No!" she replies. "We have to stay and help!"

"Tell me who this is," you repeat.

"This is Paolo, one of our collaborators. He can help you."

"Nia, we don't just have random collaborators walking around. Where did he come from? How did he get here? Besides, the only thing that will help me is getting back to McMurdo Station. Help me radio for a helicopter."

Turn to page 50.

"We can call for help, but there's a storm coming. They're not going to be able to send a helicopter. By the time you get back to the station, it will be too late to save your leg. It's really bad."

She's right. You see a disturbing collection of clouds in the distance. Helicopters do not fly in bad weather. Storms can go on for days here. Who knows when you will be able to get proper medical attention? And she's right about your leg. This type of blunt trauma can easily result in amputation, especially if you don't get to a hospital fast enough.

"But listen. Paolo and I can help you. We can save your leg." Nia glances at Paolo nervously. "There's this newly developed serum. It's going to essentially put the cells in your leg into biostasis, like *Scottnema*. But I cannot tell you anything more about it, or about Paolo."

You feel lost. You do not want to wait days for a rescue. You would certainly lose your leg. But how can you just agree to some strange treatment that she won't even explain? Besides, you are a scientist! You cannot promise not to ask questions! You trust Nia, but you do not trust this Paolo guy. Why were they sneaking out of camp in the middle of the night? They are the reason you got injured in the first place!

If you accept Nia and Paolo's treatment, turn to page 65.

If you call for a helicopter, turn to page 76.

Of course you want Lucas to live! You disagree with Nia and Lucas's methods, but you do not want to interfere when they are so close to a big breakthrough. You agree to look the other way and continue with your own research. You are walking toward your experiment when you hear Lucas call your name. "Look out!"

You look around but don't see anything and laugh to yourself. This is probably another one of his famous pranks. Then you hear him yelling again. "Run!" His voice is urgent now.

You turn slowly toward him just to show him that you are rolling your eyes. Lucas is racing toward you, panicked, but you see no sign of a threat. Then suddenly you feel a sharp jolt of pain in your knee and collapse forward, falling on top of a haggard penguin. "Ow!" Is this one of Nia and Lucas's research animals? Escaped? Zombified? "Lucas, help!" He starts to run toward you but before you know it, the penguin is on top of you. It's got the strength and vigor of a true predator. You never thought you would lose your life to an undead penguin mummy.

The End

Fighting back tears, you give Jordan's limp hand a squeeze and then climb down off the helicopter. You rush back to where you found the backpack to scour the area for clues. Just past the backpack there is a large snow drift.

As you reach the other side of the drift you see a giant hole in the ice that looks fresh. Dive holes that are left to sit in the cold air often refreeze quickly. If it's a new hole, there's hope. It means that Dr. Burman may not have been underwater for long.

You put your drysuit on and check to make sure there are no leaks. Because saltwater freezes at a lower temperature than freshwater, the seawater in McMurdo Sound is actually below freezing. Your drysuit is like a spacesuit, keeping all the water out. But even a stray hair can create a break in the seal, allowing the frigid waters to seep or flood in. This is the kind of mistake you must be careful to avoid.

You dive in, and moments later you feel a disturbance in the current behind you. You turn to see a giant submarine appear from out of nowhere! You feel a rush of water, and your body gets sucked backward. You are being pulled into the sub's airlock—a chamber separating the sub's interior from the ocean. The exterior door closes with you inside. You watch in astonishment as the water drains around you. The inside door raises, and you cautiously enter the submarine's interior.

A bright light shines in your face.

"Welcome aboard the SS *Aries*. We are federal agents. You are safe. For now."

Turn to page 54.

"Excuse me?"

"Time is short, so I'll be brief. We know you are deployed on a search-and-rescue mission for the US Antarctic Program. Your missing colleague, Amir Burman, has been . . . compromised. By interlopers. From another part of the solar system."

"Are you saying that the scientist I'm looking for has been abducted by aliens?"

A pause.

"Not abducted. He is a willing collaborator."

"I guess it's more the *aliens* part that I'm stuck on."

The agent ignores this. "We have been aware of their presence on the planet for some time, and we've tried to monitor their activity. We know they need something from us humans, and that's why they've got Dr. Burman with them. We need a mole. That's you."

"Um, no thank you?" You definitely did not sign up to spy on aliens for the US government.

"We have good reason to believe that the entire planet is in great danger unless we can stop them. But we need to get Dr. Burman out. All you have to do is proceed with your rescue attempt and wear this wire and this earpiece. We'll do the rest."

This is way too much. You're a scientist, not a spy! And you definitely do not want to get in the middle of a conflict between the CIA and . . . aliens! But on the other hand, your job is to save Dr. Burman, and this seems to be the way to do it.

If you decline to cooperate with the CIA, turn to page 69.

If you accept the mission, turn to page 70.

By the time you finish talking to Lucas and get yourself dressed, the figures are gone. However, there are some patches of snow going up the valley wall, and you see two sets of fresh footprints. You are practically running to try to catch up. The thin cold air cuts into your lungs. You reach the next snow patch and scan for the prints.

Upon a closer look, you notice some additional indentations in the snow. But they are an odd shape. You bend down. Penguin tracks? They seem to be on top of the human tracks. While there are mummified penguin and seal bodies scattered around the Dry Valleys, you've never seen a live one. How unusual. For almost an hour, you continue following a tandem path of penguin and human tracks. Suddenly, the human tracks veer left, while the penguin tracks continue uphill. Of course you know you should try to catch up with the intruders to find out what's happening, but you can't stop thinking about this poor lost penguin.

If you follow the penguin tracks, turn to page 62.

*If you follow the human tracks,
turn to page 83.*

You walk over to Jordan, put your hand on her arm, and lower your voice to a whisper. "Jordan, I know what you're thinking. But I don't think these aliens are going to remain friendly if you tamper with their . . . experiment." You nod at her dive knife, tucked next to her hip. "Listen, we already know that global warming is causing great damage—glaciers are melting, the sea levels are rising, and entire species are going extinct. Even if we stop releasing greenhouse gases tomorrow, we will remain on that trajectory. Yes, it seems crazy to introduce an alien microbe. But this could be our best chance to undo the damage we've already done. How can we live with ourselves if we don't at least try?"

Jordan sighs. "You can talk me into anything, huh?"

"Okay, then. Let's make some microbe stew." You turn to look at the Pyrathians. "We want to help you."

"Thank you," says the voice from the intercom.

Dr. Burman begins climbing the ladder and you and Jordan follow. At the top of the ladder, he reaches up and pushes a large chunk of ice sideways, revealing a sort of escape hatch in the ice.

"The higher-ups will want to talk to you right away," you say. "You'd better get your story straight."

You click your radio on. "We've found Dr. Amir Burman. He is safe and healthy. But we've all been diving, so hold off on transport till tomorrow."

Go on to the next page.

It's true that changes in altitude immediately following a scuba dive can make divers very sick. But your dive was so brief that you could safely fly right away, especially if the helicopter stays low. You just want to buy some time so that you can hike up the valley and gather microbes for the Pyrathians.

"Let's get going!" says Jordan.

"We'll be back," you say to Dr. Burman.

You and Jordan fill your packs with extra gear. "I guess we'll have to freedive in the lake. There's no way we can bring our scuba tanks," says Jordan.

"Fine, but I'm definitely using my drysuit to at least seal out the cold water. We can't risk going hypothermic up there."

You set off from New Harbor up Taylor Valley toward the lakes. You check your GPS unit every so often, as there are no paths, trails, or markers in Antarctica. Taylor Valley is part of the McMurdo Dry Valleys—a dramatic glacier-carved desert landscape, largely free of ice and snow. Instead, the ground beneath you is mostly soil, littered with rocks and boulders deposited by ancient glaciers.

The valley floor is rough, full of little mini hills, called hummocks, that make for slow, strained walking. But the views are extraordinary. Each Antarctic spring and summer, the layer of ice under the soil melts a bit, forming beautiful glowing aquamarine pools, lined with fluorescent orange and green algae. Hiking up valley, you see Lake Fryxell emerge, a blue-white glowing pool surrounded by dark soil and glowing white tips of glaciers.

Turn to the next page.

This could be a good place to gather microbes, but you aren't as familiar with Lake Fryxell. The ice on the edge of the lake is thin, so you walk along the shore instead of crossing the lake.

When you arrive at the snout of Canada Glacier where it presses up against the valley wall, your heart practically jumps out of your chest. A group of figures appears in the distance. They disappear again beneath the ridge, but you know that in just a few minutes they'll see you.

"Who is that?" says Jordan.

"I have no idea. Fryxell Camp was supposed to be vacant this season. I guess there's a group hiking down from another site for fieldwork," you reply.

There's no way to explain your presence here. You are supposed to be waiting at New Harbor Camp.

"Should we hide?" Jordan asks, sounding as panicked as you feel.

In Antarctica, the air is crystal clear. On a sunny day, it feels like you can see forever. How can you possibly hide from them? You are still close enough to the edge of Canada Glacier that you could climb up and hike on above them, out of sight. But you definitely do not have the proper gear for hiking on a glacier.

If you hike up onto the glacier, turn to page 78.

If you hike straight toward the other scientists, turn to page 87.

I can't leave her, you think. You climb up into the helicopter, and moments later the pilot takes off. Every few minutes you check Jordan's breathing and pulse. She seems stable but remains unresponsive.

The station doctor, Dr. Riley, is waiting at the helicopter pad at McMurdo, and she whisks Jordan away immediately. After an excruciating half hour, Dr. Riley tells you that Jordan's vitals are improving, but she's still unconscious.

"May I see her?" you ask desperately.

"I'm afraid not. Something strange is going on. Please tell me exactly what happened out there and what you saw."

You recount every detail your memory can muster.

"Hmm," says Dr. Riley. "I asked for this information because there is some material in Jordan's nose and throat that I cannot identify. I ran a rapid DNA-sequencing test, and the substance seems to be completely unique. We'll need to study it further in the lab to confirm. Jordan must be quarantined until we learn more. And if we resume the search for Dr. Burman, we will need to proceed with extreme caution."

Go on to the next page.

"*IF?*" You're shocked! "We have to find him!"

"Do *you* want to go back there?" Dr. Riley raises her eyebrows. "After everything you've been through?"

She's right. The whole situation is beyond creepy. A completely alien substance?

You cannot imagine going anywhere without knowing Jordan's condition. But you promised her that you would try to find Dr. Burman. If you don't go now, it may be too late.

If you choose to resume the search for Dr. Burman, turn to page 73.

If you choose to remain at the station, turn to page 82.

62

The penguin tracks lead you up the hill for another thirty minutes, and then seem to end abruptly next to a giant wind-carved boulder. You are nearly ready to give up and head home, but as you walk around the other side of the boulder you see a penguin body! It looks like it's been there for dozens of years. As with most of these mummified seals and penguins, the windward side of its body is practically a skeleton, but the other side is perfectly intact.

How could it have made these tracks?

Then all of a sudden it starts to . . . move! Its abdomen swells and shrinks rhythmically as though it is breathing. Its head swivels toward you. You reach forward to touch it and its beak snaps at your hand.

"Step back immediately," an accented voice says.

You look up and recognize the intruder from your camp.

Turn to page 64.

"I'm Paolo Esposito," the intruder says. "I am a representative from the Commission for the Conservation of Antarctic Marine Living Resources. We have observed that there are individuals here tampering with protected wildlife. I am investigating this issue. I am afraid I must cite you for violating the Antarctic Treaty, and you will be deported from the continent for this violation."

You stammer, trying to explain yourself, but nothing satisfies him. He calls your National Science Foundation representative on the radio. There is something very fishy about this person. He claims to be staying at the Italian base, but he shares no further credentials, you've never heard of him, and you have no idea where he came from. Nonetheless, he has photographs of you trying to touch the penguin, and your credibility is ruined. Your career in Antarctica is over.

The End

"Okay, you're going to feel a numbness," says Nia. You flinch as you feel the serum coat your skin and permeate your wound. Gradually, the pain subsides.

Paolo and Nia exchange words in Italian and then he sets off by himself. You want to ask where he's going, but you figure Nia won't tell you.

You begin limping after her down the hill and back to camp. The two of you almost stumble over a mummified penguin. This seems to be a new one—you've never seen it before. In fact, you could swear that it was not there just a few hours ago when you hiked up the hill. How strange. You turn to Nia. Her face is as white as a sheet. She looks panicked.

"Kind of weird," you say. "I've never seen this penguin mummy before. It's pretty far up the valley too."

"What, this one? It's been here for years." She composes herself again quickly, and you limp back to camp, exhausted. The pain is bad, but somehow not unbearable. You collapse into your tent and drift off to sleep.

Turn to the next page.

You awaken with your stomach growling. You feel ravenous. Without even checking your watch, you clamber out of your tent to look for food. As you walk toward the Jamesway, your eyes catch movement toward the lake. It's Nia and Lucas, presumably heading to their experiment site.

Hunt them. Eat them, says a voice.

Startled, you look around to see who is speaking. The phrase repeats twice before you realize it is your own voice. Almost of its own accord, your body begins moving quickly toward them.

What is going on? You don't want to eat Nia and Lucas! Yet the urge seems to grip your whole body. You pause, take a deep breath, and use all your will to suppress it. "Confused" does not even begin to describe the chaos gripping your brain.

The revelation hits you with extraordinary clarity. Nia must have derived the serum directly from *Scottnema*. You are now becoming nematode. Scientists have long understood that certain parasitic nematodes drastically change their host's behavior. One type of nematode that infects tropical ants causes them to forage far from their nest and turn red. Birds then mistake the ants for berries and eat them, allowing the worm to finally reach its end goal of infecting the bird. *Scottnema lindsayae* is not known to be parasitic. But the serum Nia applied to your leg must have enabled *Scottnema* to infiltrate your body and hijack your deepest impulses.

Go on to the next page.

Scottnema is the apex predator in terrestrial Antarctica, so it makes sense that you are now overtaken by the urge to hunt everything alive around you. You wonder if Nia could be aware of this side effect. You want to talk to her about what's happening, but you do not trust yourself to be anywhere close to her. Or Lucas, or anyone else for that matter.

Antarctica is definitely the right place to avoid human contact. If you can just survive until these urges pass, things might be okay. But that is a big if.

If you decide to head out on your own, turn to page 113.

If you decide to approach Nia and Lucas, turn to page 125.

You lock eyes with Jordan. She has a point. What makes anyone trust these aliens? Besides, there's no telling what will stop them from altering planet Earth even more. No empire stops at just one settlement. What if they transform the entire planet into an ice ocean, like their homeland?

They're not going to like what Jordan is about to do, though, so you try your best to get Dr. Burman clear of any fallout. "Look, I'm on your side," you tell him in a hushed voice, "but I'm not sure Jordan is convinced. I need a minute alone to talk to her." You feel bad making him think you're going along with his plan, but you want to keep him safe. You gesture for him to go first up the ladder. As soon as the hatch closes behind him, you signal Jordan, who slashes the reactor open.

"What have you done?" exclaims the disembodied voice from the intercom.

You do not know the answer to this question. Did you just blow your chance to stop global warming? Or did you just rescue humanity from nefarious aliens?

Suddenly, strange multicolored vapors fill the chamber. You and Jordan begin choking on the fumes and everything starts to spin. Your limbs grow weak and you collapse to your death.

The End

"Agent Combs, I can't help you. I'm not a spy."

He frowns at you for a moment before responding. "I'm sorry to hear that. In that case, I'm afraid we have to remove you from the region. We cannot allow you to remain in Antarctica. You could compromise our operation. You'll need to enter into witness protection."

"What? You can't do that to me! Besides, if I miss my next radio check-in, they'll search for me too!"

"I'll make sure the station manager knows you're with me now. He and I are old friends." Agent Combs gives you a troubling wink. "As for entering the Witness Protection Program, you could avoid that by facing a tribunal for compromising national security. But I'm guessing you wouldn't like that."

You are furious, but there doesn't seem to be anything you can do.

You follow Agent Combs to your new bunk on the sub, where you will live until you reach your new home in New Zealand.

The End

You nod, and the agents proceed to outfit you with surveillance gear. You put your regulator back in your mouth, then head out through the airlock.

You program the GPS coordinates the CIA agents gave you into your dive computer. As you proceed in that direction, you suddenly see a horde of glowing orange figures surrounding a giant, cylindrical glass chamber. The orange light emanating from each form is so blinding that you cannot look at them directly. But out of the corner of your eye, you see that their bodies are shaped like giant tadpoles with wings. Inside the chamber, you can make out a single human figure. You hold up your hands to indicate a peaceful approach.

Déjà vu jumbles your thoughts as a sudden current pulls you into yet another airlock. Before you know it, you are plopped onto dry land. The chamber is like an inverse fishbowl—dry on the inside and surrounded by water on the outside. It reaches all the way up to the sea ice above you. There is a ladder that connects the floor to a hatch in the ceiling, presumably giving access to the surface.

Go on to the next page.

The figure inside is of course Amir Burman. "I'm so glad you're here," he says. "You are the exact person I want to talk to."

"Dr. Burman, I cannot tell you how happy I am to see you. But what's all this?"

You feign surprise as he briefs you on the aliens and shares more details. You learn they are from one of Jupiter's moons, Europa, but the aliens call it Pyrath. They hope to build a settlement here in the frozen Antarctic Ocean because it is similar to their ice-covered oceans.

But they have concerns about global warming, because their species requires cold temperatures to survive. They have brought a group of microscopic organisms, known as a microbial community, from their home planet. These microbes capture gases that otherwise would heat the planet—like carbon dioxide and methane—much more quickly and efficiently than any Earth organism. Still, they had hoped to combine their microbes with some microbes from Antarctica to optimize their chances of survival here on Earth. They have been running experiments in a tank known as a bioreactor.

"I've been trying to help them with this, but I haven't had a chance to collect the Antarctic microbes they need, and now they say the US government is onto them. Some of them want to release the Pyrathian microbe as it is now, and others want to wait. I know you have studied marine microbes. Do you think you can help?"

Turn to the next page.

You don't know what to say. Noticing your hesitation, Dr. Burman adds, "This microbe could stop, or even undo, so much of the damage that we have done to the planet. We could put an end to global warming if we can help them."

Agent Combs's voice pipes into your ear, "Do NOT let them release those microbes. This is even worse than we thought. This could mean biological warfare."

You want to do what the agent is telling you to do. But what if Dr. Burman is right? You know that the government is about to step in. If you could possibly save the world by releasing the microbes, shouldn't you take that opportunity?

If you choose to assist the CIA,
turn to page 80.

If you release the microbes, turn to page 93.

As you land again at your dive site and prepare your gear, you keep looking up expecting to see Jordan. Instead, you find yourself getting ready with Wren, a lanky graduate student who you've never worked with before. It's nerve-wracking to dive with somebody new in any circumstances, let alone when the stakes are so high.

You lead him over to the spot where Jordan collapsed and see nothing but empty ice. "The backpack was right here, I swear!"

He gives you a strange look. "Maybe those GPS coordinates you took are wrong."

You feel annoyed by his skepticism. "Let's just divide the area up and search one section at a time."

You can barely focus. How are you going to manage this dive? Has it been ten minutes or ten days since Jordan's collapse?

"Over here!" Wren's voice jolts you out of your daze. You catch up to him and see he has found a small dive hole. "Why is there a dive hole here? We'd better take a look. After our friend leaves."

Turn to the next page.

A huge Weddell seal is hogging the hole from under the water. Seals here usually find cracks in the ice to breathe through, and you have to sit there and wait. The Antarctic Treaty dictates that you cannot approach or disturb wildlife without a permit.

Finally, the seal meanders away, and you plunge into the water. You exhale to initiate your descent but rather than being pulled down, you find your body is pushing upward. You empty your drysuit of air and yet somehow you are still bouncing up instead of plunging down. There is another body beneath you! The seal? No . . . it's a tangle of flailing limbs! You scramble to the ladder and heave yourself up and back onto the ice. Breathlessly you spit out your regulator and pull off your mask.

Go on to the next page.

"What are you doing here?" shouts a voice. Treading water inside the dive hole is another diver!

"Dr. Burman!" shouts Wren. "We're here looking for you."

"For me? Why?"

"You missed your check-in! The station triggered a search."

"I absolutely checked in at 0800 hours. I spoke to Josh at McMurdo communications."

"We've been trying to reach you," protests Wren. "What about all our radio calls since?"

"I've been underwater most of the day, I guess. This is my third dive."

Waiting for the rescue helicopter, you and Wren pepper him with questions, but nothing adds up. Somebody's lying. You suspect it's Dr. Burman, but he is so well-regarded he might just get away with it.

"Well, we've found you," you say, giving up. "That was our job. I guess you'll sort the rest out with McMurdo."

When you land at McMurdo, you see a handful of people wearing suits approach the helicopter. "Amir Burman, you are under arrest, for conspiring to commit acts of bioterrorism."

Stunned, you and Wren watch them hustle Dr. Burman away.

The End

"There's no way I'm going to accept this so-called treatment if you won't tell me what it is." You pick up your radio. "McMurdo comms, do you read me? My leg has been struck by calving ice. I need a rescue."

A voice crackles back, "Condition One here. Helicopter flights are grounded. Do you have access to first aid?"

"Yes," Nia interjects.

"We'll get you out as soon as we can," the voice tries to reassure you.

Go on to the next page.

Nia and Paolo support you from either side and you begin hobbling back to camp. At the very least you should be able to beat the storm. There's no sign of the mysterious bag they were hauling away. They continue to speak excitedly to each other in Italian. You do not trust Paolo.

At the bottom of the valley, you see an ATV parked on the lake's edge. The three of you decide it's best to ride in the vehicle the rest of the way to give everyone a break. As Paolo leans over to hoist you onto the seat of the vehicle, you catch a glimpse of something shiny. You freeze in terror. There is a gun tucked into his waistband!

This is all too much, you think. If you can make it to Blood Falls Camp at the other side of the lake, you might be okay. But can you really get there on your own? And how will you survive the storm? There is supposed to be another science team there, but you don't know if they've arrived yet.

If you go back to your camp with Nia and Paolo, turn to page 102.

If you peel off and head to Blood Falls Camp, turn to page 114.

Backtracking a bit, you hike up a small cliff, finally reaching a spot where the cliff is almost the same height as the glacier. You really should have crampons and an ice axe, but at least you had the foresight to bring microspikes—pieces of rubber covered in metal spikes that stretch over the soles of each shoe. You usually use them to help your feet get traction crossing the frozen lakes, but they help you stay upright on the glacier too. You move slowly and deliberately, testing each step before putting your full weight forward.

You have been hiking for hours and your pack is heavy. Your brain keeps drifting off, trying to assimilate all the strange things that have happened in the last day.

Suddenly you hear Jordan cry out, and you turn toward her. She's fallen down and is rubbing her knee. She's about a football field's length behind you—you hadn't realized how much faster you were going. You rush back toward her, confidently retracing your steps. You veer slightly as you approach her, and without warning the ground gives out beneath you. Your face slams against the edge of the crevasse and you twist backward as you fall. The cold and pain rush over you all at once. Everything turns black.

The End

"Listen to me," pipes the voice of the agent in your ear. "You and Dr. Burman have got to get out of there. We need you gone, stat. But bring the microbes with you."

You pause for a moment to take this in and try to improvise a believable excuse. "There's no way that a microbe adapted to Europa will thrive here," you tell Dr. Burman. "The Pyrathians' plan to modify them is important. I think we can get the perfect microbes from Lake Bonney. But we need to bring that bioreactor with us."

A voice comes through an intercom at the edge of the chamber. "The bioreactor stays here."

"It's the only way," you protest. "There are countless possible microbes at the lake. I cannot possibly bring samples of each back here. We'll need to see how each species interacts with these Pyrathian microbes at the lake itself. Using the bioreactor."

Lying like this makes you shudder, but you're not about to get between the government and some alien invaders.

Go on to the next page.

You and Dr. Burman set to work disconnecting the bioreactor and carefully haul it up the ladder. You trudge across the sea ice and up into the Jamesway—an elongated hut structure—at New Harbor Camp. As the door creaks open you jump, finding the same agent you met earlier waiting inside.

"Great work," he says.

Dr. Burman turns to you. "What is this?"

"I'm sorry, Amir."

"Dr. Burman, nice to meet you. I'm Agent Combs. I'm afraid your friends from Europa mean harm to the planet."

"That's not true!" yells Dr. Burman. He flings himself toward the bioreactor, trying to preserve its contents, but Agent Combs steps in his way. "That's government property."

Dr. Burman pushes through the door back outside, and you follow. He screams as you see a giant explosion emanating from the spot where you left the Pyrathians.

"You did the right thing," says Agent Combs.

Honestly, you're not so sure.

The End

Even though Jordan is unconscious for only one day, it feels like an eternity. You're so glad that you stayed put so you could be there when she wakes up. Jordan has to remain in quarantine, so you send funny notes and drawings back and forth to keep both your spirits up.

After two days, Dr. Riley arrives with some news. "We have attempted to identify the substance found in Jordan's airway but have had absolutely no success. It is a biological substance, but it is completely distinct from any known organism on the planet. The good news is, all remaining traces of the substance have evaporated from Jordan's body, so her quarantine is over."

There is still no sign of Dr. Burman. You beg the station manager to allow you to return to the site where you found the backpack that made Jordan sick. Though you have no hope of finding Dr. Burman at this point, you are desperate to get your hands on that backpack so you can study this mysterious organism!

But when you return, it is gone.

The End

The two sets of human tracks continue parallel to the lake, and you follow them for almost two hours.

After some time, the second set disappears. But you follow the remaining tracks and finally realize they are heading down the valley, toward the next camp. *I guess I'll join the big party down-valley after all*, you think, remembering the debate about where to spend the holiday.

You follow the tracks all the way past Seuss Glacier and onto the next lake. You see the neighboring field camp in the distance and pick up your pace. You will be so glad to see other old friends who are working at nearby field sites. And you are eager to determine who was in your camp at night and left these tracks heading over to the next field camp. Maybe there's a reasonable explanation. It's early morning now and you see a few familiar faces emerging from their tents. You head into the main hut and startle, seeing Nia at the table.

"Hi there," says Nia, looking equally surprised.

"What are you doing here, Nia?"

A strained chuckle emerges from Nia. "I um, I . . . couldn't sleep, so I decided just to hike over here."

"Without telling us?"

"I was going to radio you all first thing!"

Nobody is supposed to go hiking alone in Antarctica, but having just done the same thing, you're not going to give her a hard time.

Turn to the next page.

"But wait, what are you doing here?" she asks.

"I was following you! Well, I saw two people in camp. And then they disappeared. So I was following their tracks."

"You saw people in our camp?" says Nia. "That's so weird. Are you sure?"

"I'm positive." You now feel sure that one of those people was Nia, but she's not saying anything.

Nia changes the subject and picks up her radio. "I guess we better call Lucas and tell him to head out here."

You are interrupted by old friends greeting you. Everyone is helping to prepare food for Thanksgiving dinner and dressing up in wacky outfits—one of Antarctica's unusual holiday customs. You go outside and open the costume box. You put on a sequined cape and helicopter beanie and find a pile of hot dog costumes underneath. You hand one to Nia before going back into the kitchen. Fresh fruit is almost unheard of out in the field, but some of the scientists brought some from the research station yesterday as a special treat. You spend the morning making an elaborate penguin sculpture out of pineapples and berries. After a light lunch you and the others start setting and decorating the table.

Without warning, the door to the hut bursts open. It's Lucas. He's out of breath and panting.

"Lucas!" You see that his arm is bleeding. "Are you okay?"

"We need to barricade the hut. They're right behind me."

"Who is right behind you? What happened?"

Turn to page 86.

"Listen, we've been running some biostasis experiments on . . . penguins. We managed to transfer the nematode mechanisms for biostasis to penguin cells, but we haven't been able to control the reanimation process. Now they've reanimated themselves and they've become aggressive."

"Like . . . zombies?" you say.

"Yes, and there are a bunch of them. They chased me in here."

Suddenly there is a pounding sound. You can hardly believe your eyes. A penguin is hurtling itself against the window. Everyone starts barricading the door. The penguin disappears. A few minutes later the banging starts again. You look out the window and see a figure in a hot dog costume. Nia! "We have to let her in!" You begin removing the barricade.

"Stop," says Lucas. "If we open the door they'll get in and it's over for all of us."

"Are you serious?" Something tells you that Lucas is right, but how can you leave Nia out there?

*If you keep the door barricaded,
turn to page 100.*

If you open the door, turn to page 116.

There are three scientists approaching. They wave happily to you and introduce themselves.

"We didn't think anybody else was out here," says a scientist who introduces herself as Lena Reyes. You've heard of Dr. Reyes's work with water that tracks—channels of water flow just below the soil surface—but you've never met before. You try to come up with a cover story—why didn't you try to think of one before? You're a terrible liar.

Jordan comes up with a beautiful half-truth. "We just completed a rescue on the coast and now we're trying to squeeze in a little fieldwork till we get transported back to McMurdo."

Dr. Reyes gives you a wink. Everyone knows you're not supposed to "squeeze in" fieldwork without approval, but a lot of scientists understand the need to multitask. Luckily it seems like she is going to look the other way.

"We're on a boondoggle of our own," she shares conspiratorially. "We were heading to Raina's camp in the middle of the valley for Thanksgiving, but McMurdo Station says there's a storm coming and we better head to the nearest camp. So we're going to hunker down at Fryxell Camp. It's going to get here even sooner than anticipated. You'd better join us."

Turn to the next page.

You and Jordan look at each other. Antarctica has some of the strongest winds on the planet. The Dry Valleys are littered with rocks and gravel deposited by the glaciers that carved them. If you stay out in a storm, you could easily get pelted by windblown rocks. There is no way you can get to Lake Bonney and back before the storm hits. Should you try to gather what you can from Lake Fryxell and return to New Harbor before the storm takes over? Or hunker down in the Fryxell Camp hut and wait until the bad weather passes?

If you decide to dive at Lake Fryxell, go on to the next page.

If you decide to go with Dr. Reyes's team to Fryxell Camp to wait out the storm, turn to page 106.

"Hmm . . . I think we will try to get back to New Harbor," you say.

"All right, it's your call. Just stay safe out there," Dr. Reyes replies.

Her group continues on toward the Fryxell Camp hut. Once they're out of sight, you and Jordan locate a spot on the lake where you expect to find a good sample of cyanobacteria. You begin hacking at the ice with your axe and saw to create a hole.

You each squeeze into your drysuits, fins, and masks. Diving in the lake is completely different than the ocean. The ice covering the lake is typically a lot thicker, so not as much sunlight makes it through. But you can still see the vivid orange and green microbial mats that form beautiful honeycomb shapes and spires along the lake bottom, like a little fairy city.

You are much more accustomed to scuba diving than freediving. When you freedive, you don't have an oxygen tank and simply hold your breath underwater for as long as you can. Still, you find that you can stay submerged for a couple minutes at a time—long enough to find some mats of cyanobacteria that will be perfect for the Pyrathians. You are about to do one more dive to collect the mats you've spotted when you hear Dr. Reyes's voice on your radio. "Winds will be reaching thirty-five miles per hour soon."

"There's no way I'm giving up now," you tell Jordan. You complete two more dives and then get ready to race back to New Harbor.

Turn to the next page.

You need to lighten your pack, so you ball up your dive gear and stash it behind a boulder. Microspikes—rubber outsoles covered in metal studs attached to your shoes—help you and Jordan get traction on the ice and move quickly across the frozen lake.

The wind is at your back, at least. The lake feels safe because there's relatively little flying debris. But once you make it onto dry land again, windblown pebbles from the ground begin pelting you. The winds get so strong that you fall forward several times. You pause for a moment and Jordan pulls you into a miniature valley between hummocks. "I think we should wait here," she says.

"But I can *see* New Harbor. We're so close."

She shakes her head. "I'm stopping here for a while."

"I have to keep going." Forward progress has long been your motto, and you feel more determined than you ever have before.

You begin running again, and every three or four steps the wind tumbles you forward. You hold your backpack up behind your head to protect it from flying rocks. Fifty feet from New Harbor the wind changes direction and you can barely fight it. You've been running for hours. You collapse, heaving. "Amir, Amir, come in," you plead into your radio. You share your location and within a few minutes Dr. Burman appears and drags you into the hut.

You lie in the hut, exhausted, while Dr. Burman runs some DNA analyses on the samples you've brought back from Fryxell. He shares the results with you. "This one is perfect," you say victoriously.

Turn to page 92.

Dr. Burman grabs the prime sample, puts on a mountaineering helmet to protect himself from windblown rocks, and heads out to find the trapdoor leading to the Pyrathians' outpost. You want to go with him, but Jordan needs your help. You grab a mountaineering helmet for yourself and one for Jordan, and head back to where you left her. You see her crawling on the ground toward you, and you run to her and guide her back to the New Harbor hut.

You want to venture out to check on Dr. Burman and the Pyrathians, but it's too risky. The afternoon and evening pass slowly. You begin to wonder if you've lost Amir Burman for good this time. You and Jordan doze off fitfully.

Finally, Dr. Burman's voice jolts you awake as he bursts through the door of the hut. "Success!" he exclaims. "The Pyrathians were able to combine the cyanobacteria with the microbes from their home planet. The microbial mat has been released and seems to already be thriving on the seafloor here. Soon it will spread through the Antarctic Ocean."

"Let's hope it does what they say it will," Jordan replies.

The storm continues for two more days. You pass the time drafting your next research proposal: *Changes in Greenhouse Gas Concentrations Following the Discovery of a New Microbial Mat in the Antarctic Ocean.*

The End

You look at the microbes on the bottom of the bioreactor. They have already grown into a lush fuzzy mat. It looks like bacterial mats you've seen in the deep sea, but much more vibrant and luminous. It seems to pulsate with every color in the rainbow. Taking it in, you know you must help these aliens. But with the CIA on the verge of busting in, there's no time to modify the microbes.

"Tell them to hold off on releasing those microbes! We need to get in there and stop them!" Agent Combs's voice is sharp inside your earpiece.

You pretend that you cannot hear Agent Combs. You try to muffle your mic with your handkerchief. "Let's release them as is and hope for the best," you whisper.

Turn to the next page.

"What are you doing?" barks Agent Combs. "You are supposed to stop them!" You continue to ignore him.

There is a great commotion amongst the Pyrathians. They pull the bioreactor out into the ocean and set to work opening it up. But as soon as the mat meets the natural seafloor and surrounding water, it begins to disintegrate. You look at Dr. Burman and see tears welling in his eyes. "It's not working," he says.

"I'm sorry Amir, that was the wrong call. But some CIA agents are going to burst in any minute. There was no time," you whisper.

"Excuse me?" he says, aghast. "How do you know?"

You pause, wondering how you can explain your run-in with the CIA. But then a robotic voice crackles through the chamber's intercom, interrupting your thoughts. "Thank you for your help, humans. We cannot stay here. We will prepare for our return to Pyrath. You humans know it as Jupiter's moon, Europa. Would you like to join us? We can build a special chamber on the seafloor there, like this one, but with plants, freshwater, and a shelter that replicates your natural habitat. You will be very happy there. You will find it quite beautiful."

Go on to the next page.

You've spent your life studying frozen soils, frozen lakes, frozen oceans. How can you pass up an opportunity to go to Europa? But your life is here on Earth. Besides, you're not sure you trust these Pyrathians. After all, they left some sort of poison booby trap that seems to have put Jordan in a coma. Shouldn't you be getting back to the station to find out what happened to her?

"Thank you for the invitation," you say, "but I belong on Earth."

Dr. Burman looks at you pleadingly. "Are you sure? This is our big chance to explore another world."

Maybe he's right.

If you travel to Pyrath, turn to the next page.

If you stay on Earth, turn to page 111.

It's hard to imagine leaving your life behind. But in your heart you are an explorer and a scientist. How can you possibly turn down the opportunity to investigate life on Europa? Everything you find there will result in groundbreaking research. Not to mention, you are most at home in the ocean. Living under Europa's frozen seas sounds incredible. "Let's go," says Dr. Burman, his eyes sparkling with excitement.

The ground beneath you begins to rumble. You look down and realize that the chamber is part of a giant spaceship. Your chamber takes up only a small portion of it. The water around you is part of another fluid-filled chamber on the ship. Before you know it, the sea ice above you is smashed away and the ship emerges from beneath the water.

You hurtle up into the atmosphere.

The End

You have lost all trust in your colleagues. You know they are hiding a lot, and you are afraid of what they might do if they know you're onto them. You need to let the National Science Foundation representative at the station know right away, but you can't risk discussing it over the radio. You want to have an in-person meeting as soon as you can safely get back to McMurdo. Waiting out the three-day storm and playing dumb proves almost untenable. You can barely eat, sleep, or focus on your research. As soon as the winds die down and the skies clear, you fake a stomach illness.

"I think I ate an expired protein bar," you whine, coming back from the bucket toilet for the eighth time in an hour. "Shackleton's revenge, you know?" That's a nickname for food poisoning in Antarctica. Later that afternoon, a helicopter arrives to take you back to McMurdo Station. Upon return, you head straight to the NSF representative's office.

Go on to the next page.

"Dr. Povis is out in the field, at Erebus Hut. I'm her new assistant, Leif. You can share everything you need to with me, and I'll relay it to Dr. Povis."

"This is very sensitive information. I'd prefer to speak to her in person. It's urgent."

"I could escort you there by snowmobile," offers Leif.

There's something very strange about Leif. You've never heard of Dr. Povis having an assistant on the ice. You want to talk to her, but something tells you that you do not want to be driving up the side of an active volcano with this Antarctic novice. You could just file a report directly with CCAMLR, the Commission for the Conservation of Antarctic Marine Living Resources, but going around the NSF to talk to them would break protocol. The NSF would not be pleased.

If you file a report with CCAMLR,
turn to page 107.

If you travel with Leif to Erebus Hut to speak
with Dr. Povis, turn to page 119.

"What's happening?" Nia asks, stepping into the kitchen area. "I just woke up from a nap."

You do a double take. "Nia! If you're in here, who is that out there?"

You peer out the window again and see the hot dog costume receding. A gust of wind picks up and the costume collapses into a puddle, with three penguin bodies emerging from inside. Of all the sights in Antarctica, you never imagined you'd see zombie penguins inside of a hot dog costume.

You start questioning Lucas again. "Okay, what the heck is going on? You've been secretly doing experiments on penguins?" Everyone in the hut has gathered around.

"Nia has been working with me on it, too."

A chorus of voices excitedly shouts questions.

"How can you do that?"

"Why would you run these experiments here? On protected wildlife?"

"That's completely unethical!"

"It was the only way," says Nia. "We tried bringing the nematodes back to our labs in the US, but we weren't getting anywhere. We needed to try it here. Over the years we just watched for penguins that were lost, far from their rookery, that would have died anyway. We'd sedate them and then experiment with inducing biostasis. I know it seems unethical, but we could save countless lives with the technologies we are developing. Now we know we can put human cells into biostasis too. This could mean an end to so many diseases. Increasing successful organ transplants. Saving soldiers wounded in battle."

Go on to the next page.

"Why were you sneaking around camp last night?" you ask. "And who was with you?"

"That was Paolo. Obviously we have had to seek funding from other sources. Most government sources object to our work. They say it is a gray area with regard to the Antarctic Treaty, which discourages commercial applications of Antarctic research. Paolo is from an Italian pharmaceutical company. He was unhappy with the pace of our work so he came here to . . . hurry us along."

Eventually the conversation slows and everyone, somewhat stunned, resumes Thanksgiving dinner preparations. The mood is awkward. Everyone understands that Nia and Lucas will be banned from all future research in Antarctica. While you disapprove of their motives, you are inspired by their breakthroughs.

Decades later, you will accept a Nobel Prize for the impact of your biostasis research on human health. You almost wish you could share the prize with Lucas and Nia. It would never have happened without them.

The End

It's too risky to head all the way to Blood Falls with the storm moving in. You slide over to let Nia into the driver's seat. You keep your eyes trained on Paolo as he and Nia exchange words. He abruptly walks off, back toward Hughes Glacier. Nia starts up the ATV, carefully staying away from the edge where the ice has melted.

"Are you going to tell me who the heck that Paolo guy is? And why he has a gun?"

"I promise I'll explain everything, but . . . oh my gosh!" she exclaims all of a sudden, jamming on the brakes.

A mummified penguin is lying on the lake, directly in your path.

"Okay, that's new," you say. "I've never seen a penguin body lying on the lake ice like that."

Nia pauses for a moment before saying, "You need rest."

"Nia, why are you denying it? The only mummy that's this close to camp is Carla the seal. Most of the penguin and seal mummies are way down-valley. That's two new ones today!"

Go on to the next page.

"Nope, that's been there for years. Let's get you lying down." Nia steers the ATV around the penguin.

It's like talking to a wall. "Nia, you're working with an armed man, there are new penguin mummies around, and you've got some weird cutting-edge mystery medical treatment just in your bag casually? If you don't tell me what's happening, I'm going to have to call the bosses back at the station and tell them everything I know."

"Don't do that! Please! That could destroy all our careers. You're involved in this now too!"

"Involved? I don't even know what *this* is!"

You pull up to the camp. "Stay there," orders Nia, climbing out of the ATV. "I'll get Lucas." The two of them emerge a few minutes later and help you off the vehicle. They wash your wound and wrap it. The pain is excruciating. You collapse onto a cot and realize how exhausted you are.

Turn to the next page.

104

The sound of a chopper startles you awake. You look at your watch. It's midday; you've been asleep for hours. Has McMurdo sent a medevac for you? How? You know there's a storm at McMurdo and flights are grounded.

"Nia? Lucas?" you call out. But there is no response. You drag yourself to the window and catch a glimpse of the helicopter. An involuntary shudder runs through your body. The helicopter is not one of the familiar US Antarctic Program helicopters! It's dark green, like a military helicopter. You see Nia, then Lucas, climbing in. You try to call to them, but before you know it the helicopter has taken off.

You immediately get on the radio to McMurdo to ask about it, but they have no idea what's going on. The next few days pass painfully slowly. Your dreams become increasingly vivid, and reality seems more blurred.

One morning, movement outside the window catches your eye, and you drag yourself to the door. The cold wind shocks your face, and you squeeze your eyes shut. When you open them, you see a line of three haggard-looking penguins scooting past you. Is it an apparition? You struggle to follow them, but a new gust of wind knocks you flat against the rocks. You raise a hand to your head and are horrified to see it covered in blood. You collapse as your vision fades to black.

The End

106

"What's our rush, really?" you say to Jordan. "We've been racing to get back to New Harbor before McMurdo sends a helicopter for us. But they won't dispatch any flights with a storm coming in."

"True," Jordan agrees. "Let's stay here till the storm passes."

The two of you have a great time getting to know Dr. Reyes and her team. Since no scientists were expected at Lake Fryxell over Thanksgiving, there are only emergency provisions. But everyone does their best to transform the freeze-dried meals into a special dinner. Costumes are traditional during holidays in Antarctica, but since you don't have any here, you draw funny beards and mustaches on each other with markers and make hats out of sample bags.

When the storm finally dies down you radio Amir Burman for an update.

"Don't bother coming," he says grimly. "They've disappeared. I heard an explosion last night. I tried to go back to find them but the chamber we'd been using is decimated. There's a gaping hole in the sea ice and no sign whatsoever of the Pyrathians."

Your stomach seems to drop out of your body. You did not realize how much you wanted this to work out until now. You feel utterly heartbroken.

Turn to page 118.

You are awoken by a knock on the door. Your watch says 10:00 AM. You feel embarrassed to still be asleep, but the truth is you have only been drifting since filing the report to CCAMLR. You feel awful for reporting your friends, but you know there was something disturbing about their activities. You open the door, feeling sheepish. There stands a man wearing a suit beneath the standard-issue red parka.

"I'm Allan Hughes. CCAMLR sent me to investigate your colleagues. I've just returned from the field and I am sorry to say I was unable to corroborate anything you told us. Can you please explain why you filed a bogus report? You've wasted my time."

You gape at him. You can hardly believe it. Nothing you say seems to satisfy him. It's too late to return to the field. You end up heading home, having wasted a season in Antarctica. You may never again get the funding.

The End

108

You step out of the hut, your heart racing. The door slams shut behind you. Nia and Lucas are walking away, up the hill. You call after them and they turn toward you, looking startled.

"So, you've successfully put penguins in biostasis."

"You were in there?" Nia says.

"Yes. I heard everything. And I know you're violating the Antarctic Treaty's rules about experimenting with local wildlife without a permit. What are you thinking?"

"It's not what it looks like!" Lucas stammers. "Or, I mean . . . it's the only way. You know that the nematodes here in Antarctica have an exceptional mechanism for biostasis. And that we could make a huge impact on medical treatments for humans if we could only transfer that mechanism to more advanced organisms. But we can't seem to replicate any of our experiments in the lab back home in the US. They only work here. So we had to start with larger animals here in the Antarctic. We never took them from the rookery. We would just take the penguins that had already wandered away. They're doomed anyway!"

Your jaw is slack with shock. "Do you have any idea how unethical this is?"

Go on to the next page.

"It's more unethical to walk away from this!" Nia pleads. "We are so close to a breakthrough! We have a serum that can bring almost any type of cell into biostasis. We just need better control over the mechanism of reanimation."

"We could save so many lives," interjects Lucas. "We can stop the aging process. We can save soldiers wounded in battle. We can stop cancer in its tracks. Possibly cure it. We've been working with a pharmaceutical company in Italy. We have clinical trials starting there next year."

"The Antarctic Treaty System is in place for a reason. When you violate it, you threaten the work of all of us scientists here," you say. "I'm sorry. I need to tell the National Science Foundation what I saw."

"Please don't," begs Lucas.

"Look, there's a lot of money in this research," says Nia. "We have to keep it off the books, but we have a ton of cash coming in from that Italian pharma company. We could split it with you. You'd never need to apply for another grant again. Your research funding would be set for life."

"Now you're trying to bribe me? That's even worse!"

Nia looks at Lucas. "Just say it."

Turn to the next page.

110

Lucas puts his head in his hands and then looks up. "I've got stage four cancer. It's very aggressive. There's no known treatment. But if I can just run a couple more experiments this season, I feel sure this serum can save my life. Please let us keep working on this?"

How can you say no to saving Lucas's life? After all, you could just pretend you saw nothing and continue your own experiments. Reporting them would disrupt everyone's work. But on the other hand, there's no guarantee that this serum will really cure Lucas's cancer. They said they haven't figured it all out yet. Besides, your career would be destroyed if anybody else found out that you knew about this.

If you turn a blind eye and return to your own research, turn to page 51.

If you decide to report Nia and Lucas's illegal activities to the National Science Foundation, turn to page 122.

"I'm sorry Amir, I just can't do it. This is my home. Besides, a lot happened on our search. I need to make sure everything is okay."

"What do you mean?"

"Jordan was with me at the beginning. We found what I think must have been your backpack, but it was covered with a poisonous substance. She's been unconscious since she touched it."

"Sorry about our booby trap," says the voice from the intercom. "As we said, we believe your government is trying to find us and we needed some protection."

You take one last look at the glowing forms surrounding the chamber before climbing the ladder to the surface. You open the trapdoor and plop down on the sea ice, dizzy with everything that's just happened. "How am I ever going to explain that I found Dr. Burman, but then lost him again to aliens from Europa?"

"I'll take care of that for you," says a voice behind you. You didn't realize you were talking to yourself out loud. You look up to see Agent Combs towering over you. Before you know it, your hands are behind your back. "You are under arrest for resisting the orders of a federal agent. You have the right to remain silent."

"Seriously? Those aliens might have killed me if I followed your orders! You're lucky I'm alive!"

Turn to the next page.

112

Agent Combs doesn't meet your gaze. "A helicopter is on its way. From there you'll wait in the National Science Foundation office at the station until we can get you back to the US. If you want to avoid jail time, you'll stick to this story: We were investigating Dr. Burman for bioterrorism research. You refused to comply with our investigation. The end."

You glare at him as you wait for your helicopter. How can this be? You essentially just discovered intelligent life elsewhere in the solar system. Perhaps the biggest scientific revelation in human history! And you, a scientist, are supposed to keep this quiet?

But on the other hand, who is going to believe you?

The End

As quickly as possible, you stuff your pack with food and an emergency shelter. If you can make it to the coast before the storm, you can shelter there and survive by catching cod.

You scrawl a note to Nia and Lucas. "It appears that *Scottnema*, like its parasitic relatives, is overtaking my consciousness. I am now a danger to other people. I am just going outside and may be some time. I will radio if I need help. Do not search for me."

You begin your trek. The wind is picking up, but luckily it's at your back. Antarctica has always felt like home to you. You have often wondered if there was some way to live there forever. The problem was always winter. But who knows what this nematode serum can offer you? Perhaps, like *Scottnema*, you can enter biostasis during the coldest, darkest months, and reanimate when conditions improve.

You are never heard from again.

The End

You just don't trust Nia anymore. Before she can climb up onto the ATV, you reach your good foot down to the pedals and accelerate toward the other side of the lake.

"Hey!" Nia calls. "Stop! What are you doing?!"

She and Paolo start running after you, but eventually seem to give up.

You continue on toward Blood Falls, slowing down as the ice gets thin. The wind is picking up and you can see clouds moving in. Just as you reach the edge of the lake, you hear a crack and feel the ATV pitch sideways. You tumble down and the icy water immediately numbs your body. Somehow you manage to right yourself, and you splash the rest of the way to shore.

The wind fights you hard as you drag yourself up the hill. A surge of adrenaline pushes you up the hill and you find yourself almost smiling as you reach the plateau of Blood Falls Camp. But then your heart sinks as you scan the campsite and find it empty. The wind is pushing hard on you. Your body is still dripping and numb, and you collapse on the lee side of a boulder. The sun has disappeared behind clouds and the temperature is dropping quickly. Between the shock of injury and the encroaching hypothermia, your thoughts simply will not jell. You drift off to sleep, thinking of the Antarctic heroes that succumbed before you.

The End

116

You push past Lucas and begin to disassemble the barricade. Just as you open the door you hear Nia's voice behind you. "What's happening? I just woke up from a nap."

If Nia is behind you, who's outside? Suddenly the force of the door swinging open sends you flying backward. You look up and realize that the hot dog costume is filled with mummified penguins stacked on top of each other—a wobbling tower of flippers and beaks and rage! Before you know it, three of them have emerged from the costume and are pecking at you violently.

The End

118

"We made the right call," Jordan says. "We could have died in that storm. And even if we had made it back with the right samples, we might have all been killed by whatever that explosion was."

"I know, but this was our big chance to stop climate change," you say.

"We can still do that," says Jordan. "Sure, we might not have a magic microbe to help us. But like I said before, humans here on Earth created the problem. We know what we need to do to stop it."

You decide then and there that from now on, you will focus your research on curbing and capturing greenhouse gas emissions.

The End

"You know, I've never had the chance to visit the top of Mt. Erebus," you say. It's the world's southernmost active volcano and it sits adjacent to McMurdo Station, but your research has never taken you there.

"First time for everything!" Leif replies, motioning for you to climb onto the snowmobile behind him.

The view as you ascend is dazzling, and the volcano is covered in extraordinary fumarole towers. As gases vent from the volcano, the snow above the vents vaporizes and then freezes again from the cold air, forming extraordinary towers and chimneys three or four times your size.

Despite the beautiful landscape, you feel increasingly uneasy. Leif makes you nervous. From the moment you met him, there seemed to be something shifty in his demeanor.

Turn to the next page.

You start to calm down as the snowmobile approaches the hut, but before you know it, you are driving past it. The hut is receding rapidly, and you are approaching the crater! Mt. Erebus has one of the only exposed lava lakes in the world, and getting close to it can be dangerous. What is Leif doing? Why didn't he stop at the hut? You are almost to the edge of the crater, and you begin to panic. Is he trying to kill you? Anything is possible after what you've seen of your colleagues in the Dry Valleys. If you lean forward, you can reach the handbrake at the front of the snowmobile. Or you could jump off and make a break for the hut.

If you pull the handbrake, turn to page 128.

If you jump off, turn to page 127.

122

Your hands are shaking as you type the email to the officials at the National Science Foundation. It feels terrible to interfere with something that could help save Lucas's life, and the lives of countless others. But harming wildlife in Antarctica's delicate ecosystem is just wrong.

As you hit send, you feel like you are making the wrong choice. You would have been better off joining Jordan's search and rescue operation and avoiding this whole mess with Nia and Lucas.

You start walking along the lake to clear your mind, and you hear . . . a voice frantically shouting your name? Looking up, you can hardly believe your eyes. Your mind must be playing tricks on you.

"Jordan?" It's more of a question than a greeting. She's waving her arms wildly and running toward you. There's another person with her. It's Amir Burman, the missing scientist!

"I'm so glad we found you," Dr. Burman says.

"You're glad you found *me?* I was supposed to find *you*," you reply. "Dr. Burman, what happened to you? Are you okay?"

"Yes, I'm fine. I just got very absorbed in an important experiment."

That seems a bit fishy, but Jordan interrupts before you can ask more about it. "Listen, we need a big favor," she says. "We hiked up here from New Harbor. Dr. Burman has discovered a community of microbes that capture greenhouse gases far more quickly and efficiently than any other creature on Earth."

Go on to the next page.

"But there's a catch," Dr. Burman chimes in. "They come from a lightless environment. They would die off if exposed to sunlight. But to be most effective in mitigating greenhouse gases, we would want them to thrive at any ocean depth. This includes the ocean's surface, where sunlight penetrates the water. I know you're studying nematodes now, but I read your paper on how cyanobacteria pigments provide protection from solar radiation. I am thinking that if we can combine cyanobacteria with the microbes I discovered, we could truly have an impact on global greenhouse gases."

"I'm not so sure about bio-geoengineering," you say. "I don't believe in manipulating our environment. Especially in a delicate ecosystem like Antarctica. The unintended consequences could be brutal."

"That's how I felt, too," says Jordan. "But Dr. Burman convinced me. These microbes could truly reverse global warming. We don't have a lot of time. Can you please just help us?"

You already said no to Jordan once and look what happened. You take the two of them to an area of the lake where they can find some cyanobacteria. Jordan is able to freedive in the lake to collect plenty of samples.

Turn to the next page.

124

Over the next five years, Dr. Burman's modified microbes flourish and have the effect he predicted—they dramatically lower greenhouse gases. Global temperatures begin to stabilize—and then drop. The disastrous trend of increasing carbon dioxide in the atmosphere and oceans reverses!

But the impact on the food web in Antarctica is devastating. The new microbial community consumes the entire seafloor of the McMurdo Sound and spreads through the Antarctic Ocean. The ocean's sediment-dwelling organisms do not survive the shift. But would they have died off anyway, due to increasing carbon dioxide levels and higher temperatures? You will never know. You feel awful having had a hand in the loss of the species that made Antarctica's waters unique.

The End

You focus all your energy on pushing the nematode urge to hunt out of your mind. "Hey, Nia? Lucas? I need to talk to you. This sounds crazy. But I think that since Nia put that cream on my leg . . . well . . . *Scottnema* is taking over my brain a bit."

"What? You've got to be kidding," says Nia.

"I'm not. Look, we know that other nematodes can change the behavior of host organisms."

Lucas looks stunned. "Okay . . . what behavior is it inducing for you?"

"I have the urge to hunt. Specifically, to hunt you."

Nia and Lucas look at each other. "Listen, I don't think that's possible. *Scottnema* is not a parasite," Lucas says.

"Lucas." Nia's voice is hushed. "That may explain the behaviors we've seen in some of the . . . other organisms we've been experimenting with."

You feel it bubbling up again. You start to lunge at Nia but Lucas grabs you. You tumble to the ground.

"I'm calling for a medevac," says Nia. "I think I can come up with an antidote."

"You lucked out," the helicopter dispatcher says to Nia when she calls for a medical evacuation. "We're grounding all flights from McMurdo. Bad weather is moving in quickly. But there's a helicopter heading back from Pearse Valley in twenty minutes. They'll stop for you."

Turn to the next page.

126

Looking out the window of the helicopter at your beloved Dry Valleys disappearing behind you, you choke back tears. What a disaster. This is your favorite place on the planet. Will you ever get to come back? Are you even still yourself?

In front of you, the pilot signals the technician with his hand. That flicker of movement is like a switch. Your mind goes blank. The urge to hunt again overtakes you. Without thinking you dive forward, grabbing the pilot. Lucas and Nia scream and try to grab you, but it's too late. The pilot loses control of the helicopter and suddenly everyone is upside down.

No survivors are found at the crash site.

The End

You carefully bend your left leg up, take a deep breath, then pivot sideways, springing off the snowmobile. You tumble down the side of the mountain, jamming your leg into a rock. You try to stand and make a run for the hut, but Leif catches up with you easily. You are terrified.

"What are you doing?" he shouts.

"Were you trying to get us killed?" You stand, ready to push him off if you need to.

"I was just trying to give you a good view of the lava lake! You said you've never been up here before!"

He's taken off his helmet and you scan his face. Then you burst out laughing from embarrassment. "I'm sorry, I'm just a little paranoid. I've seen a lot of weird stuff this week."

He laughs and offers you his shoulder. You lean against it and limp toward the hut. You radioed ahead to Dr. Povis, so she is waiting at the table inside when you arrive. You share with her what you observed.

"Thank you for telling me all this," she says. "We actually have had some suspicions about this group, as they seem to have some mysterious funding sources. I've just been waiting for more evidence."

A few days later, you are back at your research site. It's lonely with Nia and Lucas gone. But your experiment is wildly successful.

The End

You are only a few feet from the edge of the crater now. Cold air rushes into your lungs as you inhale sharply. With as much force as you can muster you lean forward and squeeze the brake. But you've pulled too hard! The snowmobile screeches to a halt and the force of your momentum sends you flying into the air. Time seems to slow down as you find yourself, in horror, flying over the crater's edge. You see the many layers of exposed rock sweeping past your vision as you hurtle toward the glowing, roiling lake of lava below.

The End

ABOUT THE ARTISTS

Illustrator: Vladimir Semionov was born in August 1964 in the Republic of Moldavia, of the former USSR. He is a graduate of the Fine Arts Collegium in Kishinev, Moldavia, as well as the Fine Arts Academy of Romania, where he majored in graphics and painting, respectively. He has exhibitions all over the world, in places like Japan and Switzerland, and is currently the Art Director of the SEM&BL Animacompany animation studio in Bucharest, Romania.

Cover Artist: Iris Muddy is a forest pond creature and freelance visual development/concept artist living in Spain. Her curiosity for expressing life's beauty, stories, and adventures is what drives her. Her favorite activity is enjoying the outdoors on bicycle or on foot.

ABOUT THE AUTHOR

Lily Simonson is an artist and writer who collaborates with scientists at the furthest reaches of the planet. As a National Science Foundation Antarctic Artists and Writers Program Awardee, she spent three months camping and painting at remote research sites in Antarctica and scuba diving beneath the world's largest expanse of sea ice—often while dressed as a hot dog. She has also completed numerous artist residencies on deep sea expeditions, creating art aboard research ships and in the research submarine *Alvin*. Her work has been exhibited at galleries and museums throughout the US and Europe. *Choose Your Own Adventure: Antarctica!* is her debut novel.

For games, activities, and other fun stuff, or to write to Lily Simonson, visit us online at CYOA.com

GLOSSARY

This book is a work of fiction, with many facts about Antarctica's ecosystem woven in. There are also, however, some exaggerations and inaccuracies in the story. Read on to learn more, and to read full definitions of some of the terms you may have encountered in this book!

The Antarctic Treaty: A treaty that guarantees that Antarctica, which is the Earth's only continent with no indigenous human population, should be used only to promote science and peace. No countries may claim Antarctica and no military operations are allowed unless they are in support of scientific research. The Antarctic Treaty was originally signed by twelve countries in 1959. In the intervening decades, additional agreements have been added. These additional agreements, such as the Madrid Protocol, have dictated that the continent should be preserved and mineral resources must not be extracted for commercial gain. All agreements and protocols are known as the Antarctic Treaty System, which currently has 54 participating countries.

Bio-geoengineering: The practice of using living things—often plants, algae, or microbes—to modify the Earth's climate.

Bioreactor: Equipment in which a specific biological process is carried out and observed closely. Bioreactors are often used in scientific research as well as manufacturing.

Biostasis: In this context, it is used as a synonym for anhydrobiosis—a state of "suspended animation" in which an organism dehydrates itself, pausing all growth and chemical processes typically used to sustain life. The organism enters this state to endure environmental changes that could otherwise harm or kill it.

Author's Note: It is true that Scottnema's *capacity for biostasis may have enabled it to become the dominant species in Antarctica's inhospitable soils. However, its process for biostasis is not known to be unique. Moreover, while increasingly wet soils have caused* Scottnema's *population to decline, it is not thought to be on the verge of extinction.*

Brinicles: Also known as **ice stalactites** or **brine icicles**. When salt water freezes at the surface, bits of salt get pushed out, forming channels that are saltier, colder, and denser than the rest of the seawater. These channels sink downward and freeze at the edges, creating a giant icicle formation that is hollow inside and often branches off like tree roots.

Calving: When ice chunks break and fall off the edge of a glacier or iceberg.

Chemosynthesis: A process by which organisms convert chemicals such as sulfur, ammonium, methane, and carbon dioxide into sugars and other organic compounds for energy. It is often described as a parallel to photosynthesis, in which plants, cyanobacteria, and algae use sunlight for energy. Chemosynthesis, on the other hand, is often used by microbes that live in areas of total darkness, like the deep sea.

Author's Note: The process of chemosynthesis can create byproducts that may be toxic and have an impact on the environment. Therefore, deploying a chemosynthetic microbe to deplete greenhouse gases may not be as straightforward as it sounds.

The Commission for the Conservation of Antarctic Marine Living Resources, also known as **CCAMLR**, was established in 1982 as part of the Antarctic Treaty System. The commission is dedicated to preserving and protecting Antarctic marine life, including penguins.

Crevasse: A deep crack or fissure in the ground. Crevasses are commonly found in glaciers. They are often the result of the glacier moving at an increasing speed and stretching, or by the glacier encountering bumps in the bedrock below.

Cyanobacteria: A type of bacteria sometimes called blue-green algae. Cyanobacteria get their energy from sunlight, in a process known as photosynthesis. Cyanobacteria have evolved a special type of pigment to capture energy from light. Every plant and algae cell on Earth has a type of cyanobacteria inside of it, known as a chloroplast. But many other kinds of cyanobacteria can be found in lakes, oceans, and even around glaciers throughout the world.

Decompression sickness: Also known as the **bends**. The air we breathe is a mix of nitrogen and oxygen. When scuba divers are underwater, the nitrogen in their blood and tissues gets compressed by the pressure of the water and accumulates in the bloodstream and tissues. If divers return to the surface too quickly, the nitrogen can form bubbles and get trapped in the diver's body, causing them to get sick.

Drysuit: A waterproof suit that covers a scuba diver's body, including their hands, feet, legs, arms, and torso. It seals at the neck. This keeps extra-cold water from touching a diver's skin and enables them to scuba dive in extra-cold water.

Fumarole towers: Often found around volcanoes, fumaroles are openings in the surface of the Earth where magma-heated steam and gases emerge. In Antarctica, the water coming from the fumaroles freezes instantly, producing spires and chimneys near the vents.

Hyperbaric chamber: Also known as a **decompression chamber** or **diving chamber**. Patients lie inside a long tube and breathe pure oxygen that is delivered at two to three times the normal pressure of air. This pressurized oxygen helps the body remove nitrogen bubbles accumulated during a scuba dive and helps saturate the body's tissues with oxygen.

"I am just going outside and may be some time" were the last words uttered by Antarctic explorer Lawrence Oates in 1912. At the time, he had been part of Robert Falcon Scott's famous Antarctic expedition, in which a group of explorers attempted to be the first humans to reach the South Pole. The group spent five months walking from the Antarctic coast to the South Pole and back—a total of 1,532 miles—only to discover that Norwegian explorer Roald Amundsen had arrived at the South Pole five weeks prior. On the way back from the pole, Oates suffered terrible frostbite and became very weak. Concerned that he was a burden to his team, which was running out of food and resources, he sacrificed himself by walking into a blizzard. The group was only 31 miles from its destination.

Author's Note: See if you can spot where I included this sentence in this book!

Jamesway hut: Typically used in polar climates, the Jamesway is a long, semicircular hut that can be easily assembled, disassembled, and transported. The structure is comprised of a row of wooden semicircles that holds up large, insulated cloth over a plywood floor.

McMurdo Dry Valleys: Located in the heart of the Transantarctic Mountains, this area is one of the most extreme, dry deserts on the planet. The McMurdo Dry Valleys are the largest part of Antarctica not covered by ice sheets. Instead, the landscape is a mosaic of ice-covered lakes, glaciers, sandy soils, and rocky cliffs.

Microbe: An organism that is too small to be seen by the naked human eye.

Microbial mat: A collection of microbes that grow together to form a fuzzy or slimy covering. They are often found on the ocean floor, covering rocks or sediment.

Microspikes: Small chains or metal spikes that attach to the bottom of a shoe. They enable the wearer to gain traction on slick ice and snow.

Nematode: A phylum of worms, also known as roundworms, comprising more than 20,000 species. Many nematodes, like Antarctica's *Scottnema lindsayae*, can be seen only with a microscope, but some species can be as long as twenty-three feet.

Parasite: An organism that lives on or inside of another organism, called a host. The parasite diverts food and resources from the host, typically depleting the host in this process.

Shackleton's revenge is a play on "Montezuma's revenge"—a nickname given to stomach ailments experienced by visitors to Mexico, caused by the consumption of bacteria to which locals are immune. Montezuma was a famous Aztec ruler. Shackleton was a famous Antarctic explorer who led expeditions in the early twentieth century.

Single-celled algae: These microscopic organisms are made up of only one cell. Like plants, they use carbon dioxide, water, and sunlight to make energy for themselves and release oxygen.

Symbiosis: A long-lasting interaction between two species that remain in close proximity to one another. There are many types of symbiosis. When one organism depletes its host, as with some nematode species, it is a parasitic symbiosis. When two organisms benefit one another, it is called a mutualistic symbiosis.

Author's Note: It is believed that eukaryotic cells—the cells that make up plants and animals and have a structure with a nucleus and a cell wall—in fact came from a symbiosis in which Archaea engulfed bacteria. In turn, photosynthetic plant cells likely evolved from eukaryotic cells engulfing cyanobacteria. In this book, the Pyrathians' plan to combine their microbes with cyanobacteria would have echoed this groundbreaking moment in the evolution of plant cells.

Toxicology screen: A test that checks your sweat, blood, urine, and sometimes stomach contents for chemicals or drugs.

Ventifacts: Rocks or boulders that have been sculpted over time by windblown crystals of sand, dirt, or ice.